BLACKSPELL

Praise for the DARKSIDE series:

"Enough hellish mystery to have you drooling
for the next in the series"
Observer

"An exciting romp"
Daily Telegraph

"Wild and gripping . . . brilliant"
Sunday Express

"Atmospheric"
Independent

"This is a real cracker! The thrills and
chills come thick and fast"
Gateway Monthly

"Full of spine-chilling characters
and stomach-turning action"
Herald Express

"It's got more terror and thrills than
you could get your fangs into"
Liverpool Echo

"Brilliant"
Times Educational Supplement

Also by Tom Becker

Darkside
Lifeblood
Nighttrap
Timecurse

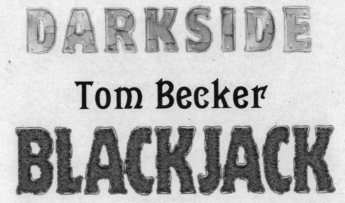

DARKSIDE

Tom Becker

BLACKJACK

■ SCHOLASTIC

First published in the UK in 2010 by Scholastic Children's Books
An imprint of Scholastic Ltd
Euston House, 24 Eversholt Street
London, NW1 1DB, UK
Registered office: Westfield Road, Southam, Warwickshire, CV47 0RA
SCHOLASTIC and associated logos are trademarks and/or
registered trademarks of Scholastic Inc.

Text copyright © CPI Publishing Solutions, 2010
The right of Tom Becker to be identified as the author of this work
has been asserted by him.
Cover illustration © Studio Spooky

ISBN 978 1407 10288 7

A CIP catalogue record for this book is available
from the British Library.

Printed in the UK by CPI Bookmarque, Croydon, Surrey.
Papers used by Scholastic Children's Books are made from
wood grown in sustainable forests.

3 5 7 9 10 8 6 4 2

www.scholastic.co.uk/zone

YA
F
BECKER
05-24-2012

For Savannah –
a dark tale for the brightest of treasures. . .

Prologue

The men came for Samuel Northwich while he was asleep: two of them, with calloused hands and whisky-soured breath. They kicked down the door of his hovel on Michaelmas Street, a fetid back alley in the bowels of the Lower Fleet, and marched up the stairs into his dark bedroom, roundly cursing Sam as they shook him awake. The boy appeared to be in a deep sleep, and when he finally stirred, his eyes remained unfocused and he seemed confused by his surroundings. His arms were wrapped round a large stone marked with a dark red stain, as though it were a child's stuffed toy.

As Sam was manhandled to his feet, clutching the piece of rubble, one of the men recoiled in disgust.

"Lawks, but this one's a bit ripe, Jacobs," he remarked to his companion. "Ain't you heard of a bath, sonny?"

"Aye, Magpie," the other man replied. "We've got ourselves a right case here."

1

"Who are you?" Sam mumbled, through cracked lips. "What do you want with me?"

"People have been complaining about you," said Magpie. "Screaming and shouting all day and all night – causing a right little ruckus. Keeping the entire street up. So we've come to take you away."

"You can't do that!" Sam protested.

Jacobs whipped out a piece of paper from his jacket pocket and waved it under Sam's nose. "Oh yes we can. We've got *documentation*," he said, proudly revelling in the word. "It's signed by one of Darkside's finest doctors. He says you'd be best off taken somewhere nice and safe, where you can shout your little lungs out to your heart's content."

"Come on, sonny," Magpie said. "Put the brick down and let's go. You won't need that where you're going."

"I can't leave it here!" Sam gasped. "It's the Crimson Stone!"

There was a shocked pause, and then the bedroom was filled with the sound of howling laughter.

"D'you hear that, Magpie?" Jacobs chuckled, wiping away a tear from his eye. "Got ourselves the Crimson Stone here!" He sketched out a mocking bow in front of Sam. "Begging your pardon, sir. Didn't realize you was *royalty*!"

"Nice try, sonny," said Magpie, not unkindly. "But take it from two rather more experienced practitioners in the art of the half-truth: you need to start your lies a bit smaller if you want people to swallow 'em. Even Jacobs here has heard of the Crimson Stone. Who hasn't?" Magpie's voice rose theatrically. "The most famous treasure in Darkside! A magical and mysterious object with the spirit of Jack the Ripper trapped inside it!" He eyed Sam with amusement. "If it actually bleedin' exists, of course, which is beyond the compass of humble men such as ourselves. If it does, though, it's a fair wager that the Stone is under lock and key in Blackchapel. Whereas what we have here – and let's be honest now – is just a mad boy with a brick."

"I'm not lying!" Sam shot back fiercely.

"Course you ain't." Jacobs leaned in closer, baring the lone tooth protruding from his gums: "Now give it here."

As he reached over to wrestle the stone from Sam, the boy wriggled and sank his teeth into Jacobs' hand. Jacobs leapt back as if he had been scalded, howling with pain.

"Right!" Magpie shouted, grabbing Sam by the collar and bundling the boy out through the door, his arms still hugging the stone. "No royal treatment for you, sonny. You can go in the back of the van like everyone else."

They frogmarched him down the stairs, Jacobs gingerly inspecting the teethmarks in his palm, and out into the deserted street beyond. It was freezing cold; wisps of fog teased the cobblestones and taunted the street lamps. A prison carriage was waiting by the edge of the pavement, a small, barred window set into the door at the rear of the vehicle.

Magpie shivered and turned up his collar.

"You've got a nerve – causing us all this fuss on a night

like this," he said reproachfully. "We're missing the party because of you."

"Party?" asked Sam, in a daze.

"You really have lost it, sonny," Jacobs said. "Hasn't no one told you? Can't you hear the cheering?"

He paused, cupping a hand to his ear. In the silence, Sam could hear the sound of a distant commotion.

"What's happening?"

"Darkside's got itself a new Ripper, ain't it? That Lucien won the Blood Succession, bumped off his sister and everything."

"Never thought he had it in him, meself," added Magpie, "what with him being a cripple an' all. But Lucien's the boss now. If you're lucky, you might see him on the way past. Now get in."

As Jacobs flung the back door open, Magpie bundled Sam into the back of the empty carriage. After slamming the door shut and bolting the bars across it, the two men climbed up to the front of the carriage and treated themselves to another celebratory nip of whisky.

"'Ere, Jacobs." Magpie nudged his partner. "Why don't I go and give Lucien the boy's Crimson Stone? Would make a lovely coronation present, don't you reckon?"

"I should think so," Jacobs laughed. "He'd be so happy he'd probably make you Abettor."

With that, Jacobs lashed a whip across the horse's flanks, and the carriage bolted forward into the night.

*

Several streets away, another carriage was moving rather more sedately through the borough: an ornate open-top vehicle, pulled by grand stallions with jet-black plumes. The carriage turned left and progressed up the Grand, where the pavements were bursting with expectant crowds. Fire-eaters spat jets of flame up into the sky while musicians played frantic, giddy tunes. Urchins hung like monkeys from the tops of street lamps, competing for the best view of the two men inside the carriage. Even the brawling street gangs paused as the carriage passed, sheathing weapons as they broke into applause. It appeared as though all of Darkside had ventured out into the night to welcome home their new ruler.

Not everyone, however, was sharing in the merriment.

"This is an utter waste of time," Lucien Ripper muttered, wincing as he shifted his position. "I have more important things to do than parade, Holborn."

Sitting beside Lucien in the open-top carriage, Darkside's Abettor kept silent. A large man with thick, snowy-white hair, Aurelius Holborn had served as first minister to Lucien's father, Thomas, for so long it had become difficult to know who was actually in charge. It had been largely because of Holborn's aid that Lucien had managed to claim Darkside's throne, but if the Abettor had expected his new ruler to be grateful, he was sorely mistaken. Lucien was in a foul mood, shaken by his brush with death only hours beforehand. During a one-on-one combat against his sister, Marianne – a long-standing Darkside tradition of determining its new ruler known as the Blood Succession – she had brought down one wall of Battersea Power Station upon them both, burying herself in rubble and nearly taking her brother with her.

Now Lucien's face was marked with cuts, and he was holding his right arm in a way that suggested it might be broken. In some ways, it was no bad thing. If he was hoping to rule Darkside, the population needed to know that he was a fighter. An unscarred Ripper would have drawn suspicion – especially one with Lucien's dubious reputation. All the borough knew that Lucien had murdered his elder brother James years before the Succession was due to take place: even in Darkside, there were some crimes considered unforgivable. That very evening the *Informer* newspaper had run an editorial pleading with the population to stay indoors if Lucien won. Holborn made a mental note to close the newspaper and punish whoever was responsible.

Lucien had been fortunate in one respect, though – Darksiders weren't foolish. Even Marianne's staunchest supporters had to know who was in charge now. It made sense to show one's approval of the new ruler, no matter how glibly it was given. And besides, few in the borough refused an invitation to a party.

"I thought this parade would please you, Master Ripper," Holborn purred. "These people are your subjects now – it is only right that you give them the chance to show their love for their new ruler. You are the Ripper, after all. This is what we planned for."

"What *I* planned for," Lucien corrected sharply. "And this

is only the beginning, mark my words." He looked over the crowds. "Only the beginning," he repeated quietly.

As he followed the Ripper's gaze, the Abettor was shrewd enough to notice subtle signs of discontent amongst the crowd. Grim-faced men stood with their arms folded, refusing to join in with the cheers; others muttered darkly in their companions' ears. Although Lucien had won the Succession, his position as the Ripper wasn't secure yet. Holborn was glad of the hulking presence of the Bow Street Runners lining the route. The giant brick golems always came alive to patrol the streets during the Succession, returning to rest once the new Ripper was crowned. But if the population proved slow to accept Lucien, they might be needed for a little while longer yet.

On the other hand, if Lucien were to be overthrown, who could take his place? The Ripper's brother and sister were both dead, and he had no heirs. Only one man could claim to have the knowledge and the authority to take the Ripper's place – the Abettor.

At that thought, Holborn allowed himself a small, private smile.

In the back of the prison carriage, Sam could hear the raucous celebrations getting louder and louder. Looking out through the barred window, he saw ghoulish, grinning faces pressing up against the carriage, and heard Magpie and Jacobs' shouts of protest as the vehicle began to rock. In the past the disturbance would have frightened Sam, but not any more. Now his mind had room for only one thing.

How long had it had been since Sam had come to possess the Crimson Stone? Days, weeks, months? Time had become so fluid that it ceased to have any real meaning. Sam dimly remembered the first time he had picked it up: the feel of the rough masonry beneath his fingertips; the shiver of foreboding as he had looked down at the red stain – Jack the Ripper's blood – on its surface. After that, everything had become a blur, a dreamlike procession. The Crimson Stone's power had consumed him, reducing his mind to the feeblest of sparks. In his more lucid moments, when the fog briefly lifted from his mind, Sam wished that he had never taken the Stone at all.

As the two men had carried him out of his room, Sam had caught a glimpse of himself in the cracked windowpane. A pair of manic, haunted eyes stared back. His face was caked with dirt, framed by lank straggles of hair, while his shirt was a patchwork of grime and sweat stains. Looking down, he saw his ribcage pressing up against his skin.

The carriage had broken free from the crowds, leaving behind the smog-ridden urban sprawl as it headed towards the quieter western edge of Darkside. The road inclined sharply, and through the bars Sam saw an imposing building standing alone atop the brow of the hill, a Gothic outline of turrets and pointed roofs. Although it was grandly elegant, there was something dreadfully wrong about the place: a sense of loss in the wild, windswept grounds; a veiled threat behind the bricked-up windows.

The carriage clattered beneath an ivy-strewn archway

and along a winding gravel driveway. As Jacobs called out "whoa", halting the vehicle outside the building's front door, a shiver of apprehension ran down Sam's spine. He shrank away as the bolts were drawn back, and struggled feebly as Jacobs hauled him down from the carriage.

"Where are we?" asked Sam.

The two men exchanged a look.

"The Bedlam," Jacobs said finally. "They'll take care of you now."

Sam's blood ran cold. "The Bedlam? You can't mean. . ."

Jacobs held up a meaty hand. "Listen, don't argue with us, sonny. We're just delivery men."

"Wouldn't catch us going inside the Bedlam," Magpie added. "We're not mad, you know."

"Neither am I!" Sam shouted.

Ignoring the boy's pleas for help, Jacobs banged the heavy knocker against the front door. It opened instantly, silently revealing a black abyss beyond.

"Please," Sam trembled. "Not here. Anywhere but here."

He shuddered as a pair of long white hands reached out from the darkness towards him. As Jacobs pushed him towards the doorway, Magpie suddenly snatched the Stone from Sam's grasp.

"I'll take that," he grinned.

A searing heat burned Sam's mind. He howled and lunged at Magpie, but there were strong, bony fingers digging into his arm, dragging him backwards. With a final desperate scream, Sam disappeared inside the Bedlam.

"Nearly there now, sir," Holborn said calmly.

The carriage had left the Grand and was now proceeding at a stately clip up Pell Mell – the broad thoroughfare that swept up towards Blackchapel, the Ripper's official residence. The wrought-iron gates in the middle of the palace's towering perimeter wall were waiting open for them, a phalanx of Bow Street Runners keeping watchful guard.

At the sight of his new home, a hint of a smile crossed Lucien's lips. The carriage moved through the gates, and was swallowed up in the darkness beyond.

1

Alone boy crossed the car park of a London hospital, beneath dark clouds pregnant with the threat of snow. He walked quickly, the wind toying with his unruly brown hair. At the main entrance to the hospital, the boy paused for a second, and then marched through the automatic doors.

Jonathan Starling hated hospitals: the harsh, all-pervasive smell of antiseptic; the dour shuffles of the patients; the pinched, worried faces of relatives in the waiting room. He hurried through the reception and up to the second floor, making for a private room at the end of the corridor. It was a relief to shut the door and look upon the patient before him.

Marianne Ripper was lying unconscious in her bed, her pale face touched with only a shade more colour than the crisp white pillows. The fluorescent dye that usually streaked her hair had drained away, leaving it a muted light-brown colour. Marianne looked peaceful, a far cry from the bleeding, shattered body Jonathan had carried through the doors of the A&E department six nights before. The attending doctor had taken one look at her and frowned – they had had to operate that night to staunch the internal bleeding.

Jonathan waited in the corridor outside, fielding a barrage of questions from doctors and the police. Who was this woman, and how had she been so badly injured? Jonathan shrugged and said that he had found her in the street, privately offering up a prayer of thanks that he had persuaded his Darkside friends Harry and Raquella to go back to his dad's house. Even though it was clear no one believed his story, on this side of London people had a tendency to lose track of Jonathan. After he'd heard that Marianne had survived the surgery, no one stopped him walking out of the hospital. Every day since he had returned to visit her; every day the staff had treated him as if it were the first time he had visited.

"No flowers?"

Jonathan looked up, startled. Marianne's blue eyes were open, and flickering with groggy amusement.

"You're awake!"

"I'm as surprised as you are. I should really be dead."

He drew his chair closer to the bed. "How are you feeling?"

"Like a building fell on me. What are you doing here?"

"It was me who found you at the power station."

Marianne raised an eyebrow. "You saved me?"

Jonathan shrugged, suddenly uncomfortable.

"I don't remember that," she said softly. "There was the explosion . . . the wall came down . . . Lucien. . ." Her eyes widened. "Lucien! Did I get him?"

Jonathan shook his head. "They thought you were dead – he went back to Darkside to become the new Ripper."

"Dammit!" swore Marianne, thumping a fist down on the mattress. "Rot him to hell!"

"Take it easy!" Jonathan said. "There'll be time to get back at him later. The doctors said you need to rest."

"Rest?" The bounty hunter gave him a piercing look. "How long have I been here, Jonathan?"

"About a week. Why?"

Marianne gingerly pushed herself up on her elbows, and tried to swing her legs out of bed.

"Wait!" Jonathan said hastily. "What are you doing?"

"I've been here a whole week? I need to go to Darkside. Lucien—"

"You need to stay in bed! The doctors reckon you're going to be here for another month at least."

In truth, the hospital staff had been baffled by their new patient. Two days after the surgery, the nurses had been staggered to see that Marianne's deep wounds had already closed over; after four days, one of the doctors had ordered they retake her X-ray results, unable to comprehend the speed with which her bones were fusing back together. Medical science wasn't to know that Marianne was a Ripper, and that her rate of recovery was far beyond that of any normal human being.

The bounty hunter slumped back down on her bed with a groan. "I can't believe getting up could hurt so much," she muttered.

"Give it some time. Wait until you're better and then we'll go back to Darkside."

"We?"

"Harry and Raquella are here too. They're staying with my dad."

"Oh? And where's your pal Carnegie?"

Jonathan bit his lip. "Lucien's men got him at the power station and took him away. I don't know where he is."

"So what are you doing here? Why haven't you gone after him?"

It was a question Jonathan had been dreading. Ever since that night at Battersea, he had been haunted by the memory of the men closing in around his friend Elias Carnegie and beating him unconscious. The fact that the wereman private detective had been taken whilst protecting Jonathan only made the image sharper, more painful. It had taken all of his friends' powers of persuasion to keep him on Lightside.

"We all want to help Elias," Raquella had said, as they sat around the kitchen table. "But rushing off back to Darkside now would be insane, Jonathan. If we even set foot there, Lucien's going to have us killed. We don't even know where Elias is, for heaven's sake!"

"It's not just that," Alain Starling said solemnly.

"What do you mean?"

"Son – we don't even know if Elias is still alive."

"Don't say that! Don't you dare say that!"

"But he's right, Jonathan," Raquella said sadly. "We need to know before we risk our lives too."

"Look," cut in Harry. "I've sent a message back over to Arthur Blake at *The Informer*. If there's any word on the street about Carnegie, he'll pick it up. Until then, the best thing we can do is sit tight and work out a plan."

"Fine. You stay here and work out a plan," Jonathan said stubbornly. "In the meantime, I'll go to Darkside and *do* something."

"That would be utter stupidity," Alain Starling said sharply. He continued, more gently: "If Elias were here, he'd say the same thing, son, and you know it."

So Jonathan had stayed in Lightside, chafing with impatience, trying to avoid the thought that Carnegie might be dead. Although no one said it, everyone knew that the wereman wasn't the only reason behind Jonathan's desire to return to Darkside. The same night that Carnegie had been captured, Jonathan had finally discovered the fate of his mum, who had been missing for over a decade. It turned out that Theresa Starling had been imprisoned by Lucien in the Bedlam, a mental asylum in Darkside – revenge for uncovering the fact that Lucien had murdered his brother. After all these years, Jonathan had finally discovered what had happened to his mum, and now he couldn't do anything about it. It was impossibly frustrating.

He had tried to talk to Alain about it – but his dad had clammed up and refused to discuss the matter. Raquella and Harry said that the Bedlam was more than just an asylum: it changed people. Jonathan didn't care. No matter what his mum looked like, or how she acted, if she was still alive he was going to get her out of there. But then he couldn't do that alone, either. . .

Marianne was still waiting for a reply. Jonathan looked down at his feet. "Why haven't I gone after Carnegie? I don't know what to do."

The bounty hunter began to laugh – a harsh, bitter sound. "And you were hoping I could help you? Look at me, Jonathan! What are you expecting me to do?"

"I thought you'd do *something*," Jonathan said angrily. "You're not just going to give up, are you?"

Marianne sighed. "Far from it. But my quarrel with my brother is a personal one. I can't afford to be running around Darkside looking for lost pets."

"Pets?" Jonathan echoed incredulously.

"Jonathan—" Marianne began wearily.

"Forget it," he retorted. "Do what you want." He got up from his chair and stormed out of the room, slamming the door behind him as he went.

Jonathan was still fuming later that afternoon, as he strode along the South Bank through the encroaching gloom of a wintry late afternoon. Although he knew it was crazy pinning any hopes on Marianne, it didn't stop her refusal to help him from hurting. After all, he had saved her life – didn't that count for anything?

A small Italian coffee shop huddled beneath a covered walkway by the Thames Path, its bright interior lights warding off the onset of evening. Harry Pierce – the young Darkside journalist, and son of the murdered James Ripper – was sitting quietly at a table in the corner, sipping from a large mug of coffee. He had managed to squeeze his broad shoulders into one of Jonathan's shirts, but it looked as though at any moment his frame was likely to burst out of it, like some sort of superhero. Unlike the other Darksiders Jonathan knew, Harry seemed to relish spending time in modern London. Given another week, Jonathan would have bet money he'd have bought a mobile phone.

Harry looked up, noting the black look on Jonathan's face. "What's up?"

"Marianne's awake."

"Oh." Harry paused. "That's a good thing, isn't it?"

"I'm not so sure now," Jonathan replied sourly.

"Didn't go so well, then?"

"She's not going to help us." He glanced around the coffee shop. "What are we doing here, Harry?"

"Waiting for someone. And if I'm not mistaken, that'll be him now."

Through the window, Jonathan saw a jittery figure

picking his way through the crowds on the Thames Path. The man was small and skinny, wearing a banded hat and a suit one size too small for him. His eyes darted this way and that, scanning the vicinity for possible danger.

"Oscar's the finest grass in Darkside," Harry said confidentially. "You want to know something, he'll sniff it out for you."

The grass slipped in through the café door and sidled towards their table, his long nose twitching constantly above a pencil-thin moustache.

"Harold," he murmured, in a soft, squeaky voice. "It's been a while." Settling into a chair facing the door, he took Harry's coffee from underneath his nose and smelled it suspiciously.

"Feel free," Harry said drily. "Thanks for coming to meet us."

"I would say it's nothing, Harold," replied Oscar, "but this part of town gives me the creeps. You know where you stand on Darkside, but Lightsiders are a rum bunch. Can trust 'em about as far as you can throw 'em."

"What about Carnegie?" Jonathan said impatiently. "Have you heard anything?"

Oscar glanced at him warily, refusing to answer until Harry gave him a reassuring nod.

"Not a bean. If the wereman's still alive, he's stashed away somewhere pretty secure. Arthur's put out all the feelers he can, but there's not much more he can do. It's common knowledge that *The Informer*'s going to get shut down sooner rather than later. You ask me, Arthur's mad not to be in hiding already."

Harry sighed. "You haven't brought cheery news, Oscar."

"These aren't cheery times, my friend. I've got a bad feeling about this new Ripper. The Bow Street Runners are still knocking about, for one thing, and those Lightside coppers too."

Jonathan's ears pricked up. "Lightside coppers?" he asked.

"Department D, they're called." Oscar twitched. "Imaginative name, eh? Anyway, that hunchback who works for them's been seen sneaking into Blackchapel a couple of times."

"Carmichael? What's he doing there?" asked Harry.

Oscar nodded sagely. "Well, that, my friend, is the question." He took a long slurp of Harry's coffee, draping his moustache with foam.

"And is there an answer?"

"Only hearsay and rumour. But an acquaintance of mine did pass on an interesting suggestion." Pulling his chair closer, the grass dropped his voice to a whisper. "He reckons that they've dredged the wreckage of that power station and they can't find Marianne's body!" Oscar chortled. "That would leave our new Ripper with a bit of egg on his face, eh? His 'dead' sister being alive and well."

Jonathan and Harry exchanged glances. "So if this is true, what are these Lightside policemen going to do?"

Oscar shrugged. "How should I know? I ain't a copper. If I was, though, I'd do the obvious things: comb the local area, pay any friends of hers a visit, check all the hospitals. . . Hey!"

He watched as the two boys leapt up from the table and sprinted out of the shop. Shaking his head, Oscar took a deep, mournful sip of coffee.

"Bleedin' Lightside," he muttered, to no one in particular.

2

In the dark, the blank windows of the hospital had assumed a strangely forbidding aspect. As Jonathan and Harry raced along the main road, an ambulance careered past them, blue lights flashing and siren wailing, and screeched to a halt in front of the main entrance. A team of medics unloaded a patient on a trolley from the back of the vehicle, and wheeled him inside.

As they approached the automatic doors at the reception area, Jonathan flattened himself against the side of the ambulance and grabbed Harry's wrist.

"Look!" he whispered.

Through the glass doors he could see the unmistakable figure of Horace Carmichael standing at the reception desk, talking to a nurse. The bright strip lights ruthlessly exposed every crease in the hunchback's shabby clothes: they looked like he had slept in them for a month. The nurse had a quizzical look on her face, but she was nodding as he spoke.

"As soon as he asks, she's going to tell him where Marianne is," Jonathan said quietly. "Do you reckon we can take him? Looks like he's on his own."

Harry frowned. "Wouldn't be so sure about that," he said slowly. "Check out those guys over there."

Peering around the ambulance, Jonathan saw two large men standing by a water cooler, silently watching Carmichael as he chatted with the nurse. Their broad frames were covered by jeans and baggy tops, hoods drawn up so that their faces were swathed in shadow.

"Hoods," Jonathan said grimly. "Only ever means one thing."

Harry nodded. "Darksiders."

"Big ones, too. We're going to have to come up with a new plan."

The nurse nodded emphatically and began pointing out directions. Carmichael glanced over towards the two men at the water cooler and jerked his head at them to follow him.

"We're out of time," Harry said, stepping out from behind the ambulance. "Looks like we'll have to distract them. I'll try to lead them as far away from Marianne's room as I can. You get up there and get her to safety. If I don't see you, I'll head back to your dad's place."

"What are you going to do?" Jonathan asked.

Harry smiled. "The usual," he replied. "Get on someone's nerves."

He turned and jogged into the reception, where Carmichael and his men were heading towards the lift.

Without breaking stride, Harry dashed up behind the two burly henchmen, grabbed their hoods and yanked them down. The men whirled round as one, revealing black, scaly faces covered in violent orange markings. Beady eyes glinted with reptilian intelligence. Harry turned pale and backed away.

It was at that moment that a nurse looked up from her chart, saw the lizard-like creatures, and began screaming. The reception area descended into pandemonium as people stampeded for the main exit. Through the throng, Jonathan saw the creatures chase after Harry down a side corridor leading away from Marianne's room. Carmichael was shouting something to the nurses, but no one was paying any attention to him. Visibly torn between following his men and finding Marianne, the hunchback paused for a second, and then headed for the lift. He hadn't taken Harry's bait.

When the lift doors had closed behind the detective, Jonathan battled his way through the crowds at the entrance, raced through the reception and took the stairs three at a time. He arrived on the second floor just in time to see the detective disappearing round the corner – in the confusion, Carmichael had gone the wrong way. Jonathan pelted along the corridor in the other direction. With visiting hours over, the hospital was quiet, the patients immersed in television programmes, music or drug-induced dreams.

Upon reaching Marianne's room, Jonathan darted in through the door and closed it softly behind him. He leaned his back against it, catching his breath. The lights in the room had been turned off, and moonlight was pouring in through the window, bathing an empty hospital bed in bright white light.

Jonathan blinked with surprise. Where was Marianne? He checked the room from top to bottom, even looking under the bed, but there was no one there. Baffled, Jonathan slipped back out into the corridor, only to hear a set of footsteps heading towards him. There was no time to hide. He froze.

When the figure rounded the corner, Jonathan relaxed. It was only a nurse. Adopting an innocent expression, he went to walk past her. But before he could react, the nurse clamped a hand over his mouth, and hauled him with surprising strength into a storage cupboard. As she closed the door behind them and pressed a finger to her lips, he saw that it was Marianne. The bounty hunter had somehow managed to change clothes, and was now wearing a light blue nurse's uniform. She was also, he couldn't help notice, smiling.

"You just can't stay away, can you?" she whispered.

"What are you doing?" Jonathan hissed. "Where did you get those clothes from?"

"Where do you think? I swapped them with a nurse."

"Oh. Right." An unsettling thought occurred to Jonathan. "You didn't hurt her, did you?"

Marianne grinned. "Of course not! She'll be fine. Once she wakes up."

"You knocked out a *nurse*?"

"I know – seems dashed ungrateful, doesn't it? Unfortunately, I got a funny feeling that it was time to go, and I felt a bit too visible in my own clothes. I left her in the toilets to sleep it off."

"You were right about one thing. Carmichael's here, and he's after you."

The bounty hunter gave him a questioning look.

"A Lightside detective – friend of Lucien."

"Ah. My dear brother has sent someone to check on my recovery. Typically thoughtful of him—"

Marianne broke off, and held up a warning hand. From the corridor outside, Jonathan heard a low hissing sound, like a tyre slowly deflating. He looked around the cupboard, searching for a weapon amongst the piles of cloths and bottles of cleaning fluid. With nothing suitable to hand, he picked up a mop.

The hissing grew louder as the creature neared. A shadow slid underneath the cupboard door, then paused. Jonathan tightened his grip on the mop, while Marianne tensed beside him. For one second, and then another, all Jonathan could hear was the hissing of the creature and the thumping of his heart, and then the shadow moved on and the creature continued along the corridor. His shoulders sagging, Jonathan let go of the mop.

"What was that, I wonder?" Marianne said thoughtfully.

"Dunno – but they've got black scaly heads, with orange stripes."

The bounty hunter's face darkened. "Fire salamanders. Nasty things – strong brutes with poisonous skin. Don't touch them."

"There are two of them with Carmichael," Jonathan said. "The other one must still be chasing Harry."

"My nephew's here? Really? If it weren't for him, I'd give up on family altogether, you know."

"You're enjoying this, aren't you?"

The bounty hunter's eyes twinkled. "I told you, Jonathan – I've rested for long enough. Now let's get out of here."

As he followed her out of the cupboard, Jonathan couldn't help but notice that Marianne was limping. For all her flippant humour, it was clear that she was still injured.

They were about to get into the lift when a faint shout rang out from the floor above. Marianne looked sideways at Jonathan.

"That sounds like my nephew. Think we should go and help him?"

They hurried up the stairs and into a brightly lit ward, hitting a tidal wave of patients flooding past them in dressing gowns and pyjamas, some in wheelchairs and others hobbling on crutches. The cause of the exodus could be seen at the end of the ward, where one of the fire salamanders had backed Harry into a corner. The young Ripper was trying to keep the creature at bay with a drip stand – the salamander hissed angrily as it ducked and weaved, waiting for the opportunity to strike.

Grabbing a wheelchair from one of the bedsides, Jonathan sent it skidding across the floor towards the salamander. The creature turned round too late, and received a sharp blow in the legs as the wheelchair crashed into it. Harry followed up by cracking the drip stand over the back of his assailant's head, sending the salamander crashing to the ground. Leaping up into the air, Harry trampolined from one empty bed to the other, keeping out of the salamander's reach.

"Nice shot," he panted, tossing the stand to one side. "Time to go, eh?"

Behind him, the salamander had already risen to its feet. Hearing Marianne cry out a warning, Jonathan turned to see the second salamander approach them from the opposite side of the ward, its black scales gleaming in the light.

"Follow me!" Jonathan cried, racing into the lift and hammering the button for the ground floor. As Harry and Marianne piled in behind him, he heard the creatures lumbering after them.

"Hurry up!" Harry shouted in frustration, as the doors closed agonizingly slowly. Behind the advancing salamanders, Jonathan saw Horace Carmichael crest the stairs and look straight at him. A flash of recognition crossed the policeman's face, and then the doors cut them off.

There was no time for relief. After reaching the ground floor, they sprinted out through the now-deserted reception and lost themselves in the crowds of frightened patients milling around in the car park. In the distance, Jonathan could hear the familiar wail of a police siren. For now, they were safe.

"Where now?" Harry asked. "Back to yours?"

Jonathan nodded. "Now Carmichael's seen me, it won't be long before Department D comes knocking. We need to get home – and fast."

3

As night fell, an icy death descended over Darkside. In the grand houses of Savage Row and Jackdaw Square, shivering masters angrily ordered their footmen to stoke up the fire in the hearth, while maids scurried upstairs to bury beds beneath layers of extra blankets; down in the Lower Fleet, families drew their rags around them and huddled together for warmth, aware that the weaker among them might not wake up in the morning.

Even in Blackchapel, the palatial home of the Rippers, freezing draughts haunted the corridors like ghosts. Outside, in the grounds, a vicious gust whipped through the air, harassing a procession as it tramped solemnly through the snow. The assemblage was dressed for mourning, the women clad in black dresses and gloves, their faces covered with lace veils; they dabbed at their eyes with small, black-edged handkerchiefs. The men wore fur coats over sombre three-piece suits, their hatbands fluttering in the breeze. Carrying lanterns to help pick out a path through the darkness, they followed slowly behind a creaking cart, upon which lay the cold, lifeless body of Thomas Ripper.

The procession headed towards a small circular building that nestled near Blackchapel's southern perimeter wall, its roof crowned by a spiked cupola. Slender arched windows were set into the granite walls, while the open doors leaked weak light on to the snow outside. Blackchapel's mausoleum had served as the final resting place for the first three Rippers. Now, with his successor decided, Thomas could finally join his forefathers.

In contrast to the pomp and circumstance of their coronations, funerals of the Rippers were simple, private affairs. Darksiders preferred not to dwell on the mortality that afflicted even their most auspicious citizens. The small crowd only served to highlight one glaring absentee – Lucien himself. The Ripper had been immersed in his throne room since the Blood Succession, leaving strict instructions that he was not to be disturbed. Whatever he was planning, he wasn't sharing it with his Abettor.

With Lucien showing no inclination to take part in his father's funeral, it had fallen to Holborn to lead the mourners. As he followed closely behind Thomas's rickety bier, the Abettor was lost in thought. He had chosen to side with Lucien for purely practical reasons – believing that Marianne would prove too strong and wilful a ruler to manipulate. Yet Lucien's mood gave him cause for concern, his sour unpredictability now at odds with the cool, calculating character with whom Holborn had first aligned.

Still, the Abettor reasoned as he ascended the marble steps leading up to the mausoleum, if gaining power caused the Ripper to lose his grip, it might well be to Holborn's advantage. Played correctly, madmen could be as easy to manipulate as a pack of cards. He would have to be careful, though – move too soon, and Lucien would be on him in a flash. Though he was a cripple, the Ripper could transform himself into the Black Phoenix, a terrifying creature cloaked in shadow and fear that could tear Holborn apart in seconds. Direct confrontation had to be avoided. It was a situation that demanded the most delicate handling, the Abettor concluded as he entered the building.

Illuminated by a forest of burning candles, the Rippers' mausoleum was an exquisite shrine to malevolence. The walls were hewn from rare red marble, the whirling patterns in the mineral resembling veins and arteries, as though the inside of the building were flesh and innards. Those who made the mistake of looking up to the ceiling were confronted by exotic friezes of murder victims, whose artistic merit was matched only by their anatomical accuracy. A series of low arches ran along the back wall, framing the separate entrances to the Rippers' tombs. The centre of the room was dominated by a statue crafted from obsidian, a dark mineral famed for its piercing strength. It depicted a cloaked man with a dagger raised aloft in his hand, ready to strike: Jack – Darkside's first, and most terrible, ruler.

The bier was brought to a halt underneath Jack's statue, Thomas's lifeless eyes staring up at his great-grandfather. As the mourners formed a quiet semicircle around the body, Holborn held out his hands in greeting, and began to speak.

"My dear friends, we have gathered here this night to witness the final rites for Thomas Ripper, our merciless and feared ruler. May—"

There was a loud crash, and the doors to the mausoleum were flung open.

"Hell and damnation!" a voice snarled.

Lucien Ripper hobbled up the aisle, ignoring the shocked murmur that greeted his entrance. Masking his surprise, the Abettor slipped into a low, graceful bow.

"Master Ripper. You honour both us and your father with your presence."

Lucien tossed an uninterested glance in the direction of the bier. "My father would have quite happily strung me up on the Tyburn Tree. He cursed my very name. The maggots can have him, for all I care."

Holborn delicately cleared his throat, and turned to the other mourners. "I think it would be for the best if the Ripper were left alone to pay his respects to his father. You shall have your chance after he is finished. Thank you all for coming."

Stifling an undertow of complaint, the mourners stood up and began shuffling for the exit. As the mausoleum emptied, Holborn pushed the large doors shut, leaving himself and Lucien alone. The Ripper paced across the marbled floor, his limp more pronounced than ever.

"Is there a problem?" enquired Holborn.

Lucien gave him a cold look. "You could say that, Abettor. Carmichael just sent word from Lightside. He found my sister. Alive."

"Why didn't he take the appropriate measures?"

"He was stopped by Jonathan Starling." Lucien limped over and pushed his face close to Holborn's. "The boy you assured me was dead."

The Abettor blinked with surprise. "Starling is still alive? I left him at your late brother's graveside in front of a firing squad."

"They missed," said Lucien, through clenched teeth.

"My apologies, Master Ripper. It appears I underestimated the boy. He does possess a certain amount of . . . persistence."

Lucien spat out a curse that echoed around the mausoleum. "Does it not occur to you, my valued Abettor, that if my sister miraculously rises from the dead and begins walking around Darkside, then my victory in the Blood Succession might just come into question?"

"Perhaps we might be able to turn this situation to our advantage," said Holborn, scenting an opportunity. "If you tell the population that there is a conspiracy threatening the throne, we can keep the Bow Street Runners out in Darkside until they've rounded up all your enemies."

Lucien sat down on the plinth beneath Jack's statue, his

face creased in thought. "You may have something there, Abettor. This would fit with a new tax I am going to introduce."

Holborn frowned. "I don't follow you, Master Ripper."

Lucien walked over to the bier and looked down at his father's body, his face stained with contempt. "Since I was a baby, my father told me that I was too weak to succeed him. There was no way that a cripple could run Darkside. He was a broken man after my brother's death. I even believe he would have favoured Marianne over me – a *woman*." Lucien shook his head. "But at the same time, the older my father got, the weaker his rule became. Do you remember the tales of Darkside's first days, Abettor – when Jack the Ripper smeared the borough on to London's map like a grimy fingerprint? Back then, its citizens were little more than slaves! Terrified of the cruel wrath of their ruler, they worked their fingers to the bone to enrich him. Since then, Darksiders have grown soft and pampered. They need a reminder of how tough life can be. My reign will provide that."

"With a tax?"

"As you said, it is only right that Darksiders show their appreciation of their Ripper. From now on, everyone – men, women, children – will have to pay me five pounds a month. We could call it . . . a conspiracy tax. Anyone who fails to pay will be considered a conspirator, and dealt with accordingly."

Holborn could barely believe his luck. There was no way that Darksiders would put up with such a brutal new tax! It sounded as though his suspicions were correct – Lucien's mind really was slipping.

"This is both a strong and a wise course of action, Master Ripper," he said, bowing.

"If I want your approval, I'll ask for it," Lucien replied icily. Raising his head, he called out: "McNally!"

There was a rumbling sound from beneath the floor of the mausoleum, and then the solid surface became suddenly fluid, a fountain of pebbles and stones cascading into the air. With a thunderous roar, the fountain solidified into the shape of an upright figure whose skin was composed entirely of masonry. Brick McNally was the leader of the Bow Street Runners; a full head taller than the other brick golems he commanded, he towered over Holborn and Lucien like a house.

"My lord?" he asked, in a deep bass that spewed out soot over the mausoleum floor.

"It turns out that my sister is still alive on Lightside – along with a boy called Jonathan Starling. They are grave enemies of mine, and a direct threat to the throne. If they so much as look at Darkside, I want to know about it. If they dare to creep back here, I'm relying upon the Runners to kill them. Do you understand me?"

McNally inclined his head, a movement that caused a loud grating sound. "I understand your order, Ripper. But the Blood Succession is ended. It is time for the Bow Street Runners to return to our rest in Blackchapel."

"Listen to me," Lucien hissed. "You'll stay out on the

streets until Marianne and Starling are found. I am the Ripper and my word is your law. And one other thing. I am introducing a new tax. Five pounds a head, payable every month. Anyone who refuses to pay is to be rounded up and placed in the Blackchapel cells. You will enforce this. Do you understand me?"

McNally nodded impassively.

"Good. Now get out of here and find Starling and my sister!"

The Runner dissolved into a ripple of stone that slipped back into the floor and rumbled away through the ground.

"He's a capable man," Holborn said. "He won't let you down."

"It would be good if I could say that of at least *one* of my men," Lucien replied pointedly.

As Holborn watched Lucien limp away and out of the mausoleum, it was hard to keep the smile from his face. Looking up at Jack's obsidian face, he winked.

"It has begun," he said.

4

The bus inched its way north, weaving in and out of the early-evening traffic. While Harry and Marianne talked in low, urgent tones, Jonathan stared silently out of the window, ignoring the wailing of a baby and the music seeping out of the headphones belonging to the girl next to him.

As they stepped off the bus at the end of his road, Jonathan saw the lights burning brightly underneath the drawn curtains in his front room. They walked through the crisp darkness and up the driveway, their breath making frosted patterns in the air. Jonathan told the others to wait for him in the hallway, then entered the lounge.

The room had successfully drawn up its defences against the winter night: curtains and lamps warding off the dark as a crackling fire repelled the cold. Alain Starling was sitting in an armchair, quietly leafing through a book. At the table, Raquella was sewing, biting her lip in concentration. They looked up as Jonathan entered the room.

"Hi, Dad – sorry I'm late."

Alain took off his glasses and clasped his hands together. "You missed dinner. Where've you been, son?"

"Me and Harry had to meet someone, and then we had to go to the hospital. . ."

"You didn't have time to phone me and let me know?"

Given the daily danger he had faced in Darkside, Jonathan found it funny that his dad could get hung up about phone calls and missed meals. Secretly, though, he quite enjoyed it. Like the warm atmosphere of the front room, there was something reassuring about Alain's parental concerns.

"I'm sorry. It really was an emergency – we had to get Marianne out of there. There were some creatures after her. It got pretty hairy."

"Did you manage to rescue her?"

"I'd like to think that I would have made it out anyway," Marianne said, striding into the front room. She flashed Jonathan a dazzling smile. "But I'm awfully grateful nonetheless. Pleased to meet you, Mr Starling."

Alain calmly acknowledged Marianne, apparently unruffled by the appearance of a strange woman dressed as a nurse in his living room. Harry came in and plonked himself down alongside Raquella, who gave him a warning glance before returning to her sewing. Unperturbed by the maid's frostiness, Harry gave her a beaming smile.

"I wonder what Carmichael told those coppers who turned up at the hospital," he laughed. "Erm . . . no salamanders here. Honest! These guys are just really, really ugly."

"He'll think of something," Jonathan said darkly. "When we fought Lucien at Greenwich, Carmichael went on the news and said we were environmental protestors. He'll say anything if it covers up Darkside stuff."

"This Department D has got me thinking," Marianne said, perching on the arm of a chair. "You want to know if Carnegie's alive, but going back to Darkside right now probably isn't the wisest thing in the world. These policemen are right here in Lightside – wouldn't it be worth asking them?"

"Excuse me, Mr Salamander," said Harry mockingly, "but by any chance have you seen a friend of ours?"

"There are ways of asking questions, nephew," Marianne said meaningfully.

"What – are you going to help us now?" asked Jonathan.

"After your rather grand exit from the hospital, I had a think," the bounty hunter replied, "and concluded I might have been a bit hasty in refusing. I get the distinct impression that rescuing Carnegie would put my brother's nose out of joint – which is enough reason for me to lend a hand."

Harry clapped his hands together. "Sounds like we've got a plan, then."

"Without wanting to butt in," Raquella said, not looking up from her sewing, "how do you propose finding these policemen? I'm presuming they don't advertise where their office is."

The room fell into silence, and then Jonathan cleared his throat awkwardly.

"But that's just the point. We don't have to look for them." He crouched over by Alain. "Listen, Dad – there's something I've got to tell you."

Alain carefully closed his book and placed it to one side. "Why do I get the feeling I'm not going to like this?"

"When we were at the hospital, Carmichael recognized me. He's got my name and my details from that stuff with the Crimson Stone over the summer – it's only a matter of time before he turns up here."

"And I'm guessing that his approach may differ slightly from normal police procedure?"

Jonathan nodded. "The house isn't safe, Dad. We need to get out of here."

Alain gestured around the front room. "You want me to leave my own house?"

"I'm really sorry."

"Are you?" Alain said, his voice rising. "We can't go to Darkside because Lucien Ripper will have us killed. We can't stay in our home because the police are coming after us with God knows what else in tow. Elias is gone. Theresa is still missing. Tell me, Jonathan, how is this going to end?"

It was Marianne who answered him. "Either we die, or they do."

"You'll have to forgive me if I don't think much of the choices," Alain snapped.

"I will forgive you," Marianne replied calmly. "But you

and Jonathan made your choices a long time ago. He didn't have to go to Darkside, and you didn't have to send him. You're players in this game now – it's too late to pull the sheets up over your head and pretend nothing's happened."

Alain looked as though he was going to say something back, but instead he simply sighed and got up from his chair.

"Where are you going, Dad?"

Alain turned in the doorway. "To pack. I'm presuming we won't be back for a while."

Jonathan peered through the net curtains at the dark, empty street outside.

"Thanks for putting us up like this."

Behind him, Mrs Elwood – the diminutive family friend of the Starlings, and near neighbour – made a dismissive noise. Since welcoming the Starlings and their friends into her home, the tiny woman had been a bustling model of hospitality: making up spare beds and producing endless plates of food, all the while her ponytail of long blonde hair swinging across her back like a pendulum. A Darksider by birth, it was obvious that Mrs Elwood could tell the origins of her new guests. Mistrustful of anything to do with the rotten borough, she pursed her lips but said nothing.

"You know I'm happy to do anything to help you and your father," she said now. "Though what on earth he thinks he's doing sitting outside in the freezing cold, I don't know."

Jonathan smiled. His dad was keeping watch in Mrs Elwood's car, waiting to follow the detectives when they arrived. Marianne was sitting beside him in the front passenger seat. Much to her amusement, the airy bounty hunter had been quick to earn Mrs Elwood's disapproval, and had swiftly volunteered to keep Alain company on his stakeout.

"Seen anything?"

Jonathan looked up to see Harry and Raquella standing beside him.

"Nothing yet," he replied. "But they'll be here, all right."

"Perhaps sooner than you think," Raquella said. "Look!"

A brown car had turned off the main road and was slinking up the street, its headlights turned off. It moved slowly past the houses, as though it were a dog sniffing out a scent.

Harry whistled. "Didn't take them long to track you down, did it? Wonder if the salamanders are still with them?"

"Doesn't look like it," replied Jonathan.

The brown car came to a halt outside the Starling house, and the driver turned the engine off. Horace Carmichael climbed out of the passenger seat. A younger man got out of the other side of the car, shivering in the cold. Jonathan recognized him as Sergeant Wilson – Carmichael's junior.

The two men walked up the driveway and rang the doorbell several times. Getting no response, Carmichael checked the darkened windows, then began working at the lock as Wilson kept watch. Within seconds, the door was open, and Jonathan took a sharp intake of breath as the detectives crept into his house. Imagining the intruders rummaging through his family's things, Jonathan had to fight the urge to run after them and throw them out.

He was suddenly aware that Mrs Elwood had joined them by the window. The little woman's face was pale, and her hand was over her mouth.

"Are you OK?" asked Jonathan. "Mrs Elwood?"

She started. "Sorry, my dear?"

"You look like you've seen a ghost."

"It's Alain, that's all. I know how upsetting watching this will be for him. I find it upsetting myself."

Touching his arm, Mrs Elwood hurried out of the room.

Although no lights came on in the house, half an hour elapsed before Carmichael sloped back out through the front door with Wilson. For all that time Jonathan remained transfixed at the window, a lingering sense of dread washing over him. From the next room, he heard the sound of Mrs Elwood murmuring strange prayers to herself.

As Carmichael's car pulled away from the kerb and down the street, the headlights of Mrs Elwood's car flicked on and the vehicle pulled out after them smoothly. As the procession disappeared from sight, Jonathan felt his nerves begin to ease.

"That Carmichael gives me the creeps," Harry muttered. "I'm not sure jumping him is going to be that easy."

Jonathan gave Harry a sly grin. "Who said anything about Carmichael?"

5

By the time that Sergeant Charlie Wilson realized he was in trouble, it was too late.

He was fighting his way through the Christmas crowds in a department store on Oxford Street, having taken the day off work to buy his family presents. Even after living in London for years, he was still amazed by the breathless, ill-tempered press of people pushing and shoving into one another, swearing as shopping bags banged into their legs.

Wilson manoeuvred towards the escalator, stifling a yawn. The previous night he had been dragged out of bed by Detective Carmichael to raid a house in north London. Apparently Jonathan Starling was still alive and well, although the only evidence Wilson had seen of that was an empty house. The sergeant was starting to lose patience with the murky world of Department D. An idealist, Wilson had joined the police force because he had wanted to catch criminals and stop crime – but now it seemed as though everyone was a criminal, himself included.

As he travelled up the escalator towards the menswear section, he felt a pair of eyes boring into the back of his neck. Wilson looked up to see a boy leaning over the railings, calmly watching him. Dismissing him as just another bored teenager, Wilson got off the escalator at the second floor. He was thumbing through hangers of jumpers when something made him look up. The boy had followed Wilson through the store and was now leaning against a mannequin, still staring straight at him.

The skin prickled on the back of Wilson's neck – a sudden premonition of danger. This was ridiculous, he scolded himself. All this nonsense about Darkside was making him edgy. He was a police officer, for pity's sake! He thought about walking up to the boy and asking him to explain himself, but then looking at people wasn't a crime. Instead, Wilson slipped between the clothing racks and made his way back to the escalators.

At the sparkling white perfume counters the sergeant paused and craned his neck to see if the boy was following him, ignoring the strange looks he received from the impeccably dressed sales assistants. In this part of the store, the air was draped with a sweet aroma.

"Looking for a present for a lady, sir?"

Wilson jumped. He spun round to see a beautiful woman smiling helpfully, displaying a small glass vial in her hands. There was something familiar about her face, but for the life of him Wilson couldn't think where he'd seen her before.

"Er, no," he said hurriedly. "I'm fine, thank you."

"Are you sure? This is a *very* special perfume, you know."

"I told you, I'm—"

Before Wilson could finish his sentence, the woman pressed down on the top of the vial, casting a fine mist of scent into the air that settled on the sergeant's skin like dew. He wanted to tell the woman off for spraying him with perfume, but the scent had made him feel pleasantly light-headed, and it seemed rude to shout.

"It's nice, isn't it?" she asked. "Makes you feel happy."

Wilson nodded, suppressing a sudden giggle.

"Excuse me," he heard a new voice say coldly. "I don't know who you are, but you don't work here."

The woman gave a silvery laugh and wrapped an arm around Wilson. He wondered why she was being so friendly – beautiful women weren't usually this nice to him. "Of course I don't work here! I was just playing a game with my boyfriend."

The assistant leaned in closely towards Wilson, a suspicious look on her face. "You don't look too well, sir. Would you like me to call for a doctor? Or security, perhaps?"

"He's fine, aren't you?" the other woman said smoothly, launching another liberal dose of perfume into the air. It was all the sergeant could do to nod dumbly in agreement. "He's not one for shopping at the best of times – bless him. I don't think you need to worry about us any more."

The assistant looked as though she was going to argue, and then frowned. She had a look on her face that suggested she had forgotten something very important. Without another word, she turned round and began talking to another customer. The beautiful woman took Wilson by the arm and led him away.

"Phew!" she whispered in his ear. "That was a close one! I thought that busybody would never go away."

At the back of his mind, Wilson knew that something was terribly wrong, but his mind was still plunged in the rich scent of perfume. He allowed himself to be taken through the store, to where the boy from the menswear section was waiting for them.

"Nicely done," he murmured to the woman.

"Why, thank you, nephew," she responded brightly. "I must confess, I've had practice at this."

"It shows. Now let's get this guy out of here. He's starting to look a bit dodgy."

The conversation swirled above Wilson's head like clouds. He recognized the words the two people were saying, but couldn't put them together in any way that made sense. Every sentence was a giant anagram. The lights and the background music and the people around him were all melding together in one happy explosion of sight and sound. Wilson had the dreamy sensation that all of this was happening to someone else, that he was merely watching as another Wilson was walked briskly towards the exit.

"Trouble?" the woman said sharply to the boy, who was glancing over his shoulder.

"Couple of security guards giving us funny looks. We need to get out of here."

"Take his other arm."

Wilson felt himself being almost hoisted into the air. Part of him wondered whether this was entirely normal, or whether he should say something to the security guards, but he didn't want the happy feeling or the beautiful woman to go away.

As they passed through the main doors and out on to the pavement, the fresh air hit him like a slap in the face. The first pangs of panic gnawed at his brain.

"What's going on?" he mumbled.

The woman was looking anxiously up and down the street, while the boy watched the department store exit. Suddenly a car screeched to a halt beside them – before he could protest, Wilson was bundled into the back seat alongside his two companions.

"Drive, Alain!" the woman snapped, and the car shot out into the traffic.

"No – stop!" Wilson cried out.

There was a heavy blow to the back of his head, and he felt himself spiralling into unconsciousness.

When Wilson awoke, the intoxicating perfume had gone, leaving him with a searing pain in his head and a parched mouth. He ran a tongue over his cracked lips, and forced heavy eyelids open. Immediately he groaned with pain – a bright light was flashing straight into his eyes, setting the nerves in his head on fire. Wilson tried to cover his face with his hands, only to discover that he was tightly bound to a chair, cords biting into his wrists and his ankles.

Shaking his head to clear the cobwebs, Wilson tried to squint beyond the light, but all he could make out was a dark, windowless room. There was a noise from somewhere in the darkness, and he realized that he wasn't alone.

"Sore head?" a voice said.

As she approached, Wilson saw that it was the woman from the department store. But whereas before she had been a kindly, comforting presence, now her pale face was set and there was a steely glint in her eyes. She was holding a small dagger in her hand. His head now painfully clear, Wilson recognized her instantly.

"Marianne!" he gasped. "But I saw a wall fall on you. . ."

"And yet here I am," she replied grimly. "Persistent, aren't I?" She nodded at the silhouette standing on the other side of the room. "This is Harry. He's family too – which also makes him a Ripper. You're not having a very good day, are you?"

"W-Why I am here?" Wilson stuttered. "What do you want with me?"

Marianne absent-mindedly ran a hand through his hair, and tapped his cheek with the flat of her blade. Wilson squeaked with fear.

"Answers," she said mildly.

Harry stepped forward and joined his aunt's side. Though

he was only a teenager, the boy was well-built and carried himself with a menacing air of confidence. He folded his arms.

"We're going to ask some questions, and you're going to be very helpful, or there are going to be problems. Do you understand me?"

Wilson nodded frantically.

"Leave him alone," a third voice said softly from the gloom.

The Rippers stopped in their tracks. Marianne rolled her eyes as Harry looked behind him, shielding his eyes against the light.

"But we haven't even started!" he protested.

"I've seen as much as I want to." A boy moved out from the darkness into the light. "Hello, Sergeant Wilson."

Wilson stared, dumbstruck, and then broke into hoarse, mirthless laughter. "Of course. I should have guessed. Hello, Jonathan."

The boy pulled up a chair and looked him straight in the eye. "Look, you're in a lot of trouble here. I don't want you to get hurt, but I don't know whether I can stop them. We're looking for a friend of ours, and we think you know where he is."

With that, things began to fall into place for Wilson. "You mean Carnegie."

"Is he still alive?"

Wilson paused, and then nodded. "They're holding him in the cells underneath Blackchapel."

Harry swore softly. "I don't fancy breaking him out from there. That place is a fortress."

"Is he OK?" Jonathan asked anxiously.

"I wouldn't know," Wilson replied. "They don't let anyone go down there, let alone me. But I did hear Carmichael talking with Holborn about keeping him alive – something to do with the Night Hunt."

There was an exchange of blank looks around him.

"What's a Night Hunt?" Jonathan asked.

Wilson laughed bitterly. "Don't ask me – Carmichael never tells me anything. All I know is, it's happening tomorrow night in Darkside, and they don't expect your friend to survive it."

"You'd better not be messing us around on this," Harry said threateningly, bunching his fist.

"It's the truth, I swear! You can beat me up all you want, but I don't know anything else!" Wilson shouted. "I'm sick of this! Sick of you, and Carmichael, and Darkside! I wish I'd never heard of the bloody place! All I wanted to be was a normal copper."

"In Department D?" Jonathan said wryly.

"If you let me go," Wilson shot back, "I'll put in for a transfer tomorrow. I swear on my family's life. If I never hear about Darkside again it'll be too soon."

His words hung heavily in the silence.

"Well, he's convinced me," Jonathan said finally. "I think we can call off the interrogation."

"Jonathan," Marianne began, "we've kidnapped a

policeman! Do you really think it's a good idea to let him go?"

"I don't think Wilson's going to be talking to anyone too soon. What else are we going to do? Keep him down here for ever? Kill him?" Wilson's eyes bulged with fear. "Even if he does blab, it's not as though we're going to be around anyway."

"You mean. . .?"

Jonathan nodded. "Back to Darkside. It's time. We'll drop him off somewhere remote and then cross over."

Marianne sighed wistfully and put away her knife. "You get less fun by the day, you know that?"

As the three of them turned to leave the room, Wilson called out disbelievingly, "You're really going to let me go?"

Harry broke into a grin. "What can I say? We're the good guys."

Jonathan paused in the gloom. "You can do one thing for me, though. When you see Carmichael, you can tell him where we've gone or not. That's up to you. But pass on a message from me."

"What's the message?"

"You're next," Jonathan said darkly.

6

In a townhouse on a quiet street in Darkside, the vampiric banker Vendetta stared moodily out through the window, watching the snow as it tumbled down from the night sky. Save for the faint orange glow of the street lamps outside, no lights were on. The darkness lapped over the vampire's skin like bathwater.

He had been sitting in the same chair for hours, barely moving. Even in a year that had thrown up one setback after another, the last week had proved particularly galling for Vendetta. He had tried – unsuccessfully – to stop Lucien claiming the throne, thereby placing himself in direct opposition to the new ruler of Darkside. Even worse, Holborn had held on to his position as Abettor. Holborn and Vendetta had spent decades nurturing a mutual contempt for one another – each mistrustful of the other's power and influence over the Rippers – and now the Abettor had the perfect opportunity to destroy him.

With time running out, Vendetta had taken what steps

he could. He had fled Vendetta Heights before Lucien's men came for him, seeking the solace of his private townhouse. Only one other person in Darkside, his maid, knew of this address – and he hadn't heard any word of Raquella since the night of Lucien's succession. For the time being, then, the vampire was safe. But he couldn't hide for ever.

To rub salt into the wound, in Vendetta's absence Holborn had moved into the Heights and set up residence. The very thought of the Abettor sleeping in his private quarters, eating meals at his dining table, and leafing through the books in his library inflamed the vampire's lifeless veins with rage. He knew that he had to strike back – but at present he lacked the money and the manpower. The obvious solution was to visit his bank and ransack the vaults, but he was certain that there would be men waiting for him there. Though Vendetta feared no one, he wasn't foolish enough to presume that he could win a battle against a squad of Bow Street Runners. As long as Lucien ignored tradition and kept the Runners on the streets, any full-frontal assault was doomed to failure.

Over the years, Vendetta had taken the precaution of storing money in accounts with Lightside banks, giving him the option of crossing over and starting a new life there. He had spent enough time on the other side of London to fit in easily enough. But as what? In Darkside, the name Vendetta was known and feared across the borough, used by mothers to threaten unruly children. On Lightside, he would be nothing: a minor businessman, little more than a shopkeeper. An eternity of mediocrity beckoned.

With each passing day, he channelled his frustration into anger at Raquella's absence. Although he had come close to draining her on more than one occasion, the maid had been the one servant he had maintained over the years. He had become accustomed to her unassuming presence, at times even favoured her with some of his thoughts. And the truth was, he needed counsel more than ever, and she was the only person left he could rely upon.

With Raquella gone, Vendetta had to do everything for himself. This would had been vexing enough at the best of times, without the increasingly problematic issue of feeding. Unable to access his money or contacts, Vendetta had been reduced to stalking the Lower Fleet for victims, hiding in the shadows like a common footpad, wary of intervention from the Bow Street Runners. The only people walking the streets at that time were usually homeless urchins or the deranged elderly, whose thin blood was little more than gruel. Even now, drowsy with hunger, Vendetta felt himself slipping into unconsciousness.

He was awoken by a knock on the door.

Vendetta's eyes snapped open. The snow was coming down faster now, submerging Darkside in a blizzard of white flakes and obscuring the front step from view. Vendetta hungrily ran a tongue over cold lips. Either Holborn had managed to track him down already, or someone had chosen the worst possible moment to pay him a visit. He moved soundlessly from his chair and into the hall. As his starved system sensed the blood pumping through the human on the other side of the door, Vendetta's teeth began to tingle. He opened the door, preparing to strike.

"Hello," Jonathan said.

For the first time in his life, the vampire was lost for words.

"You?" he managed.

"Yeah. Let us in, will you? It's freezing out here!"

The boy's shirt and waistcoat were doused in snowflakes, and he was shivering. Recovering his poise, Vendetta gave a mirthless impersonation of a smile. Perhaps this week would provide him with some satisfaction after all. He stepped to one side and made a welcoming gesture.

"By all means, Starling."

"Cheers."

Jonathan stepped past him into the hall, blowing on his hands.

"I'm surprised you managed to find me," Vendetta said, his fingers itching to wrap themselves around the boy's neck. "I wasn't aware anyone knew of my current whereabouts."

"I told him, sir," a female voice replied. Vendetta whirled round to see Raquella standing in the doorstep. "I hope you can forgive me, but I had no other choice."

The vampire snarled with fury. "I should have known! Wherever Starling shows up, my loyal maid always tends to follow."

A silhouette loomed at Raquella's shoulder.

"Don't blame her," said Harry Pierce. "If there was anywhere else we could go, we would. Believe me."

"Him as well?" Vendetta spat at Raquella. "Is there anyone in Darkside you haven't told about this place?"

"Vendetta!" Marianne cried from the pavement, stepping out from the shadows and into the light beneath a street lamp, her hair dyed a brilliant blue. She waved with mock bonhomie. "So good to see you! I believe you know Alain?"

A thin, older man was standing beside her. The vampire recognized Alain Starling all too well. It had been Alain who had turned Vendetta's feeding knife upon him over a year ago, nearly ending his life. Alain stared back at him unafraid, a look of cold contempt on his face. Vendetta hissed and took a step towards him, only for Raquella to catch his arm.

"Wait, master, please!" she implored. "These are dark times for all of us. We have a common foe in Lucien. If we fight amongst ourselves, we have no hope. But if we throw in our lot together. . ."

"And what makes you think I need your assistance?" Vendetta asked icily.

"Even you can't do this on your own, sir."

For a long time no one moved, Vendetta's gaze remaining locked on Alain. Then the vampire broke away, and led them inside the townhouse.

They sat down to an uneasy council of war in Vendetta's study, the atmosphere thick with tension. The vampire listened idly to Jonathan's story, seemingly uninterested in their escape from the hospital and the snaring of Sergeant Wilson. Only at the mention of the Night Hunt did his eyes light up with malice.

"Well, well, well," he chuckled. "Carnegie really has outdone himself this time. There hasn't been a Hunt in decades."

"You've heard of it, then?" Jonathan asked.

"Starling, Lucien's great-grandfather – Albert Ripper himself – asked me to take part in one. All the most powerful figures in the borough are present at a Hunt."

"I wouldn't hold out much hope for an invitation this time," Marianne said lightly. Vendetta ignored her.

"Sadly, I was attending to business on Lightside – retrieving a loan from an old business acquaintance – and so was unable to attend. Somewhere here, however, should be a book written by a man who did."

The vampire rose gracefully from his seat and crossed the study to a set of bookshelves, where he began running a finger down the leathery spines. "Thankfully, though I have been forced to leave behind most of my library in the temporary care of the Abettor, some of my books are here. Yes, here we are."

Vendetta pulled out a small, scarlet-bound book and glanced at the cover. "*Confessions of a Night-Hunting Man*, by Barnaby Alibi. I knew Alibi well – a weak, nervous excuse for a Darksider, with an exaggerated sense of his literary worth. This Night Hunt must have happened about eighty years ago, when Albert was on the throne. He was a brutal man, even by the Rippers' standards."

Looking up at the vampire's smooth, ageless face, Jonathan had a sharp reminder that he was in the same room as a creature of the undead. He sat in silence as Vendetta began to read aloud.

July 17th, DY 38

For weeks Darkside had been ablaze with the proclamation that the traitorous Abettor Sully Porter – the vile knave who had attempted to poison Albert Ripper while he slept (if there exists a more base and cowardly method of assassination, then it is beyond the knowledge of this writer) – was to face the trial of the Night Hunt. The men and women on the Grand could talk of little else, even if most knew that they stood no chance of taking part. However, thanks to my role as Blackchapel scribe and recorder, a black invitation fell through my letter box two nights before the Hunt was set to take place. Just the sight of Albert Ripper's signature was enough to make me shiver with anticipation.

That night I made my way to the highest ridge in Bleakmoor, dressed in blood-red riding gear. A parade of braziers lit my path, taking me to a camp in a state of frenzied preparation. Wine was flowing freely, and the air rang with bawdy choruses. The very best of Darkside society was present: Baroness Abattoir, Honved della Rosa and Jorg Gomorrah. All, however, paid due deference to Albert Ripper – the titanic ruler of our borough, who sat on his steed with the same consummate ease and majesty with which he occupied the throne. Giant blacksmiths, their exposed arm muscles bulging in the firelight, struggled to control the hellhounds that would lead the chase as they strained at their chains. In their slavering jaws I saw the gateway to eternal damnation.

When the shackled Porter was displayed before the hunters, the hounds bayed hungrily, joined by the men themselves in an unholy harmony. The prisoner was asked if he had any last words – he said nothing, his face paler than a ghost. A coward to the last. As the horses whinnied and bucked with impatience, Porter was freed and sent on his shambling way into the night. After the traditional twenty minutes had elapsed, Albert put a horn to his lips and gave it a deafening blast: the Night Hunt had begun.

Of the chase, I confess to seeing little. A novice rider, I stood no chance of keeping pace with the hunting pack. I remember the thundering of hooves around me, the unerring progress of the horses through the darkness, the distant snarling of hellhounds. As I trailed behind the other riders, from

*far away I heard the discordant blowing of a horn –
the signal that our quarry had been hunted down.
The talk around the campfires afterwards was that
Albert himself had won the chase, furiously beating
his mount in order to strike the killing blow. There
was even a rumour – whispered in the softest, most
cautious of tones – that the Ripper had wrestled with
one of his hellhounds for the privilege of taking first
bite from the disgraced Abettor's body.*

*The rest of the night was lost to drink and song.
The next morning, what remained of Sully Porter's
ravaged corpse was displayed on the Tyburn Tree, a
stark reminder to its citizens that, even in Darkside,
not all crimes can be forgiven, nor all sins remain
unpunished. . .*

Vendetta snapped the book shut. "In short," the vampire
said, "Carnegie is a dead man."

7

The procession began after nightfall, a rowdy crocodile of Darksiders careering through the streets. Drawn from the most exclusive parts of the borough – from the leafy opulence of Savage Row and the snooty delights of Lone Square to the extravagant comforts of the Cain Club – they were a rogues' gallery of thieves, gamblers and murderers. Ordinarily, they navigated the streets from the safe confines of a carriage or a hansom cab, but an invitation to a Night Hunt was confirmation of one's wealth and social pre-eminence: it was a time to be seen.

The hunters did their utmost to ensure that they were noticed. Dressed in scarlet riding gear, they swished their hunting whips at passing urchins for sport, laughing uproariously. Spotty youths tossed gold coins into the gutter, sniggering at the violent scrummage to claim them. Ordinary Darksiders bit their tongues and stayed their hands on the hilts of their weapons, unwilling to risk interfering with such a time-honoured tradition. Instead they memorized the faces of those mocking them, preparing to settle scores at a more convenient opportunity.

As the hunters continued north, the street lamps ended and the cobbled streets of Darkside gave way to the wild slopes of Bleakmoor. Usually a barren scrubland, the moor was coated in a thick white layer of snow that crunched underfoot. Flaming torches marked out a path up the hillside towards the dark, undulating ridge that dominated the skyline. Ravens flapped overhead, cawing loudly.

The hunters puffed and panted up the hillside, their faces ruddy with drink – unaware that they were being watched. Crouching down behind a giant rock overlooking the torch-lit pathway, Jonathan and Raquella maintained a chilly lookout. Having taken up positions several hours before nightfall, their thick woollen overcoats were struggling to protect them from the arctic winds. Jonathan breathed on his icy hands, his teeth chattering.

"If we don't move soon I'm going to freeze solid," he muttered.

Raquella put a finger to her lips, her cheeks reddening in the wind. If she was feeling the cold, she was too proud to show it.

"Hush!" she urged in a whisper. "We're badly outnumbered here. If anyone sees us, we're in big trouble."

"Might not be such a bad thing," Jonathan replied, shivering. "At least a chase would warm me up."

Raquella cast an eye over the stream of Darksiders still stumbling up the hill. "It won't be long now. Most of the great families have passed by. We have to wait for stragglers, remember?"

Jonathan peered out over the rolling landscape. He had heard enough tales of Bleakmoor from Carnegie to know that this was not the place to be wandering around at night – a hunting ground for wights and wild cats, the hills were said to be littered with corpses.

"I hope everything's ready," he said pensively.

"Don't worry about that," replied Raquella. "Marianne knows what she's doing."

They had parted company at the edge of the moor, the bounty hunter leading Alain and Harry off into the gloom, laden down with lengths of wire and sticks of dynamite. The plan was a hasty one, finally agreed after a night's worth of argument in Vendetta's townhouse. Lacking the numbers to take on the hunt face to face, Jonathan and Raquella's task was to infiltrate it, and hope that Marianne could provide a distraction large enough for them to get to Carnegie before Lucien did. Vendetta had steadfastly refused to provide any assistance, contenting himself with some barbed comments before retiring to his room. It was a measure of how slim their chances of success were that Jonathan found himself wishing that the vampire was alongside them now.

"Your master wasn't much help," he grumbled.

Expecting the maid to leap to Vendetta's defence, Jonathan was surprised when Raquella nodded.

"It will take him time to come round," she said. "Vendetta is not used to working with other people."

"It's his choice," Jonathan replied sourly. "If he doesn't want to work with us, he could always try his luck with Lucien."

The last of the hunters stomped past them, loudly cursing the thickness of the snow. Five minutes passed by, then ten. Jonathan was wondering whether they had left it too late when he heard the sound of footsteps ploughing hurriedly through the snow, and then a high-pitched nasal voice rang out.

"This is all your fault, Portia!" a boy whined. "If we miss the Hunt I shall never forgive you! Mama will hear about this!"

"Oh, do be quiet, Wilbur," a girl snapped back. "Your whining gives me an intolerable headache. I'm going as quickly as I can."

Two children Jonathan's age rounded the curve. The boy was glaring daggers at his sister from underneath a riding hat several sizes too large for him. Portia was daintily picking her way through the snow, vainly trying to spare her boots from the slush.

Jonathan gave Raquella a grim smile. "We're in luck," he said.

He slipped out from behind the rock and crept after the children, the sound of his footfalls drowned out by their bickering. As he got within striking distance, he pulled out a long cosh from his belt. Despite a lengthy tutorial from Marianne in how to knock people unconscious, Jonathan felt very uneasy. He needed the boy's clothes, but he didn't want to actually hurt him.

"But I want to see that disgusting mutt die!" Wilbur wailed.

Instinctively, Jonathan brought the cosh sharply down on the boy's riding hat, and was rewarded with a stifled grunt as Wilbur slumped to the floor. Portia spun round, her mouth open in shock, her boots forgotten. At the sight of Jonathan, cosh raised in the air, Portia's eyes rolled up in her sockets and she fell into a dead faint on the snowy slope.

Raquella joined Jonathan's side, shaking her head at the sight of the two prone siblings.

"I mean, *really*," she said disparagingly, dragging Portia's body behind a row of gorse bushes. "A night out in the open will do these two a world of good."

Following the maid's example, Jonathan hauled Wilbur out of sight and hurriedly exchanged clothes. As he stepped back into the torchlight, he felt faintly ridiculous in his tight jodhpurs and riding jacket. At least his hat fitted him more snugly than it had Wilbur. Leaving the two children wrapped up in their overcoats, Jonathan and Raquella hastened up the hillside, relieved to feel the blood running through their veins again.

On reaching the top of the hill, they found themselves on the edge of a campsite ablaze with activity. The hunters had congregated amidst the glow of three giant bonfires, sparks spitting high into the night air as old friends were saluted and tall tales retold. Above the din, a band of gypsy musicians were playing a delirious reel, their violins spiralling over the top of banging drums that urged the listener to stamp his feet. On the far side of the camp, away from the bonfires, a corral of hellhounds pawed at the ground, snarling with impatience. They were watched over by a contingent of Bow Street Runners, their chain leashes looking like pieces of string in the hands of the golems.

As Jonathan and Raquella stepped cautiously into the deafening hubbub, they were greeted by a paunchy man who jovially stuck a goblet beneath Jonathan's nose.

"Drink up, young 'un," he ordered. "You're a man tonight."

Unwilling to draw attention to himself by refusing, Jonathan took a deep swig from the goblet. As the scalding liquid inflamed his throat he coughed, tears springing to his eyes. The jovial man laughed and slapped him on the back.

"That's the ticket!" he cried, wheeling back into the throng.

Jonathan's eyes were still watering when suddenly, through the flames, he saw the new ruler of Darkside. Lucien was standing in the centre of a ring of hearty hunters, his slight frame dwarfed by the larger men. The Ripper looked uneasy in the glare of the attention, his crooked stance betraying his permanently crippled left leg. When an attendant tried to brush some snowflakes from Lucien's jacket, he angrily swatted their hand away. Holborn, standing a protective half-step behind, smoothly stepped in and dismissed the attendant.

Clasping Raquella's hand, Jonathan drew back into the shadows and stealthily worked his way to within earshot of the Ripper.

"Do you think we could begin now?" he heard Lucien icily remark over the crackling flames. "If one more of these drunken imbeciles tries to curry favour with me, I'll set the hounds on all of them."

"Of course, sir." Holborn bowed smoothly, and then cried out: "Bring the prisoner before us!"

At once the campsite subsided into a hush – the chatter stopped and the gypsy musicians put down their instruments. Two Bow Street Runners appeared on the ridge, on either side of a tall, familiar figure. Breathing in sharply, Jonathan watched as his friend came into view.

Elias Carnegie shambled into the campsite, his hands and feet shackled in heavy iron restraints. His shirt was torn and in tatters, his trademark stovepipe hat a crumpled mess. Angry bruises on his flesh betrayed the fact that he had been beaten. Despite his injuries, the wereman's head was defiantly unbowed. When one of the Runners brought him to a halt before Lucien and Holborn, Carnegie surveyed the cream of Darkside with a look of undisguised contempt.

"Elias Carnegie," Holborn proclaimed. "You have been found guilty of attempting to pervert the course of the Blood Succession, in the hope of preventing the true victor from taking the throne."

The wereman snorted loudly, and spat a sizzling globule of phlegm into the snow. Ignoring him, Holborn continued his speech: "This villainous attempt to meddle in the affairs of the Rippers cannot go unpunished. Tonight we take vengeance in the name of not only Lucien, but his hallowed forefathers Thomas, George, Albert and – of course – Jack."

The silence in the campsite was shattered by Carnegie's harsh laughter.

"This is a farce," he growled. "Jack would turn in his grave if he saw the human sputum now sitting on his throne."

Lucien lunged forward and cracked Carnegie in the face with his riding whip. The wereman didn't flinch, ignoring the trail of blood running down his cheek. Jonathan had to bite his tongue to stop himself crying out.

"Anything else you'd care to share with us?" the Ripper said, his voice ragged with hatred. "Any last words, wolfman?"

Carnegie thought for a second, then threw back his head and unleashed a piercing howl so loud it seemed to echo off the stars. From the other side of the camp, the hellhounds joined in, sharing the deafening lament with a kindred spirit. Finally, the howls died away.

"Enough of this," rapped Lucien. "You will be hunted down like the mongrel you are. I only hope it will be me who strikes the killing blow. Free him!"

As one of the Runners unlocked Carnegie's restraints, the wereman rubbed his chafing wrists and stretched his muscles. Holborn brought out a solid gold pocket watch from his jacket and inspected the dial.

"You have twenty minutes before the hounds are set loose. May the Rippers curse your every step."

Instead of running away, Carnegie stood stock-still, his eyes fixed on Lucien. There seemed to be a promise of sorts in his gaze. After what seemed like an age, the wereman turned on his heel and walked slowly from the campsite until the night swallowed him up.

Jonathan felt himself breathe again. The crowd's earlier jollity had been replaced by a sombre mood. As the musicians struck up another tune, Lucien and Holborn began an intense conference. The Ripper was gesturing angrily after Carnegie, his face creased with rage.

"He looks furious," whispered Raquella.

"Carnegie has that effect on people," Jonathan said, with a half-smile.

Eventually the Abettor nodded reluctantly, and cupped a hand to his mouth.

"Let us begin! Bring in the horses!"

Jonathan checked his pocket watch incredulously. "He can't start yet! It's only been five minutes!"

"Since when has Lucien played fair?" replied Raquella. "No one can escape Bleakmoor in twenty minutes anyway. It's down to us, now." She caught her breath, and when she spoke again, there was a note of wonder in her voice. "Oh Jonathan, look!"

A pack of horses had come trotting into the camp: muscular black stallions with flaming manes of yellow, red and blue hair. Their eyes were bright with an intelligence Jonathan had never seen in an animal. Even he had to admit, there was something gloriously regal about the way the horses moved.

"What are those things?"

"Night Mares," Raquella replied. "The most fabled steeds in Darkside."

As the hunters began to mount up, Jonathan cast Raquella a dubious look.

"I don't know how to ride a horse!"

"You don't need to know," hissed Raquella. "Just hang on and don't let go – they'll do the rest."

A Night Mare had stopped in front of him, its bright yellow mane blowing in the wind. Placing his foot in one of its stirrups, Jonathan awkwardly swung up on to the horse's back. The Night Mare's powerful flanks twitched, as if affronted by the clumsiness of his ascent. It tossed its head and snorted, jets of air spraying from its nostrils.

With the hunt assembled, Lucien raised a twisted bronzed horn to his lips and blew, sending a strangled, jarring note into the night. The Runners released the hellhounds, who raced out of the camp on Carnegie's trail with a ravenous joy. The Night Hunt had begun. Taking a deep breath, Jonathan kicked his heel into his horse's flank, and charged forward after his friend.

8

The Night Mare plunged into the darkness after the hounds, hooves pounding through the snow. Jonathan bounced violently in the saddle, only his desperate grip on the reins preventing him from being unseated. As the horse sharply threaded its way through frosted gorse bushes, he realized Raquella had been right – if he could just cling on, the Night Mare would take care of them both. Even as he fought to stay on its back, Jonathan marvelled at his steed's combination of intelligence and raw power.

The hunt galloped across the broad hillside: a malevolent, thunderous brood. Some of the riders hunched low in the saddle as they spurred their mounts forward, while others stood up in their stirrups, brandishing swords above their heads and filling the air with whoops and war cries. Others held aloft flaming torches, the light picking out their horses' bright manes. Far away to the south of the moor, the streets of Darkside were sprawled beneath them, mapped out by twinkling street lamps. In the midst of this wild, primeval chase, the rotten borough looked a beacon of civilization.

Though his Night Mare had settled into a fierce gallop, the more experienced riders were already leaving Jonathan behind. He was aware of Raquella riding alongside him, a look of determination etched on to the maid's face. In the distance, the hounds snarled with desire as they pursued Carnegie's scent.

The hunt veered right, heading towards a gully at the bottom of the hillside. They picked up even greater speed as they descended, so Jonathan didn't see the drystone wall looming out of the darkness until the last second. He felt the mare's muscles tense, and then suddenly they were flying in a majestic arc over the wall, landing on the other side without breaking stride. The impact sent Jonathan toppling sideways – hanging frantically on to the horse's neck, he managed to stay in the saddle and right himself as his steed pressed on down the hillside.

The leaders of the hunt had come to a halt at the bottom of the gully, their horses milling around in the shallow waters of a brook. Hellhounds pressed their snouts to the banks of the river, yelping dismally. In the middle of the throng, Lucien was cursing as he angrily scanned the hillsides for traces of movement. The hunt had lost Carnegie's trail.

As they neared the brook, Jonathan reined in the Night Mare, mindful of keeping as much distance between himself and the Ripper as possible. Although he had only been riding for a matter of minutes, his arms and legs were already aching. It was a relief to slow to a trot and sit back in the saddle.

From upstream, there came a triumphant howl.

"The hounds have picked up the scent!" roared one of the hunters, his riding hat adorned with bloodstained feathers. "The wereman has doubled back on himself, heading for the ridge! Onwards!"

Kicking his mount sharply in the flanks, the man urged the horse upstream along the brook, its hooves splashing through the water. A cry went up from the hunters, their blood thirst renewed. Geeing his Night Mare into a gallop, Jonathan exchanged a worried glance with Raquella. There was no way they were going to be able to keep pace with the hunt – the riders were too experienced, their horses too fast. Even now they were navigating the steep incline as easily as if it were flat. Unless Marianne provided her distraction soon, Carnegie was doomed.

Thundering back up towards the ridge, the hunt made for a sparse wood of fir trees clinging to the hillside. Ahead of them, the hellhounds howled with excitement as they bounded into the copse; they were closing in on their prey. The leaders of the hunt were about to follow suit when a loud explosion went off among the trees, and a ball of fire rose into the air.

As the hellhounds closed in on him, Carnegie knew that he was going to die.

The wereman wasn't scared. A lifetime spent courting death meant that it held few fears for him. In many ways, it was a miracle he had survived this long. Ever since his capture at Battersea, he had been a dead man. Lucien's men had drawn it out for as long as possible, but Carnegie's fate had been common knowledge among the grim gaolers in the depths of Blackchapel, and the wretched prisoners who shared the wereman's cell. By the time he had been hauled up to Bleakmoor, Carnegie had been sorely tempted to sit down in the middle of the campsite and wait for the end to come, ruining the Ripper of his sport. Even in death, perhaps a victory of sorts would have been possible.

So why hadn't he? Why had he loped away, making for the nearest stream in the hope of throwing the hellhounds off the scent? Why was he now scrambling through this infernal wood, branches and brambles tearing at his skin? The truth was, although Elias Carnegie may not have feared death, he didn't hate life enough to roll over and die. Anything that wanted to kill him was going to have to earn the right.

But as the howling grew louder, he knew that the time of reckoning was fast approaching. For all his vast knowledge of Bleakmoor's terrain, amassed over a lifetime's roaming the hills in both human and animal form, Carnegie couldn't outrun the hounds for ever. There might have been more fitting places to die, the wereman supposed – at a card table in a smoky tavern, or a street brawl on the Grand – but the harsh wilderness of Bleakmoor called to the beast within his soul. It would serve as a final resting place.

Then, from behind him, there came a loud boom, and a blinding light, and Carnegie realized that he might not be alone after all.

As the sky lit up and the ground trembled underfoot, the Night Mares at the head of the hunt reared up with fright, sending their riders tumbling from their saddles. A blazing orb of fire shot up above the treeline like a comet. The night rang to shouts of alarm and horses' squeals. Amidst the chaos, the hunters who hadn't been thrown to the ground reined in their horses, unsure whether to help their fallen comrades or continue the chase.

At the rear of the hunt, Jonathan's nostrils were overwhelmed by an acrid concoction of gunpowder and seared animal flesh. Reining in his horse, he saw two hellhounds come slinking back out of the trees, their snouts blackened and hides burned.

Marianne's "distraction" had consisted of a line of explosive charges dug into the ground. A decade of combat had given the bounty hunter a strategic sense that was second to none – having spent hours poring over maps of Bleakmoor, she had correctly anticipated the wereman's escape route and planted the charges at the fringes of the trees.

"Jonathan!" hissed Raquella suddenly.

Twisting in his saddle, he saw that the maid had reined in her Night Mare.

"What's wrong?"

"It's my horse," she called back. "I think it's gone lame. I'll go after Marianne and the others. You get Carnegie!"

Jonathan nodded, then urged his mount up the hillside and through the disorderly remnants of the hunt at the wood's edge. As he swept past, Jonathan saw Lucien being dragged to his feet by the Abettor, the Ripper's riding outfit dappled with sooty snow. Lucien looked up with astonishment as he recognized Jonathan.

"Stop that boy!" he cried out hoarsely.

Startled, the remaining riders hesitated before springing forward to obey their ruler. Jonathan had a slender lead over them, but his cover was gone. As he entered the copse, he knew that if he didn't find Carnegie, they were both done for.

The trees were still smouldering in the aftermath of the blast, burning branches cracking off from the trunks and toppling into the wet snow. Waves of heat rolled out from the heart of the explosion. Although a thick grey curtain of smoke hung in the air, the Night Mare weaved in and out of the trees with ease, its footing sure even in the slush. Jonathan felt increasingly comfortable on the back of his steed, as though horse and rider had formed some sort of unspoken connection.

The rumble of hooves was all around him now. Through the smoke, he could see the silhouettes of his pursuers, and flashes of scarlet riding gear. From out of the gloom there came a metallic singing sound; instinctively, Jonathan ducked, as a blade swung through the air where his head had been and bit into a tree trunk. A huntsman had drawn alongside him – cursing, the Darksider had to rein in his horse as he struggled to free his weapon from the trunk. Jonathan steered his Night Mare sharply to the right, leaving the huntsman in his wake.

Things were getting serious. Carnegie was nowhere to be seen, and Jonathan was in danger of getting surrounded. There was a twanging noise, and an arrow flew narrowly over his shoulder. Jonathan cried out with alarm, forcing the Night Mare into another abrupt change in direction. They began a precarious zigzag through the heart of the wood, arrows peppering the air around them. Jonathan lay flat in the saddle, burying his face in the bright yellow mane of his steed.

They had reached the far edge of the wood when Jonathan realized that he had been outflanked. The huntsman with the bloodstained feathers was waiting for him astride his mount, a large axe in his hands.

"Nowhere to hide, lad," he called out. "Ready to die like a man?"

The hunt was drawing ever closer behind Jonathan – the only way out was past this man. Taking a deep breath, Jonathan pulled out his cosh and spurred his Night Mare into a charge, screaming at the top of his lungs. In reply, the huntsman raised his axe above his head in a two-handed grip. Before he could bring it down on Jonathan, a scraggy hand reached up from behind the man and pulled him sharply from his mount. The huntsman yelled with surprise as he lost his grip on his axe. Falling to the floor, he was set upon by a grizzly, snarling figure, who knocked him out with one punch.

"Carnegie!" cried Jonathan.

The wereman got to his feet slowly and gave Jonathan a craggy grin. "Aren't you meant to be the one saving me, boy?"

"I'm doing my best! Come on!"

Carnegie bounded up into the saddle, and the two of them rode out from the trees and out on to the open slopes of Bleakmoor.

As they galloped to the top of the ridge, Jonathan risked a glance back over his shoulder. The Night Hunt had descended into anarchy. Riderless Night Mares were cantering across the hillsides, some being chased by hunters unwilling to trek home on foot. The blaze in the wood was still going strong, sending clouds of smoke billowing into the night sky. Aimless arrows still pierced the night sky, but no huntsmen had followed them out of the trees, and Lucien and Holborn were nowhere to be seen.

Jonathan laughed with triumph, and urged his horse onwards to safety.

9

The sun had risen half-heartedly over Darkside, as if unsure it was worth the effort. In the dingy warren of the Lower Fleet, a single ray of light cut through the clouds of smoke, catching upon something metal on the back of a rickety cart. It was a saucepan, balanced precariously atop a pile of bric-a-brac: broken furniture, battered copper piping and chipped plates. A mangy horse dragged the cart over the cobblestones, every weary clop only serving to hasten the animal towards the grave. At the head of the vehicle, two men sat beside one another – one with his head bowed, cradling something in his arms, the other staring glumly ahead as he held the reins.

Jacobs was in a miserable mood. Normally a happy-go-lucky man, he had been in a miserable mood for days, and the source of his unhappiness was sitting right next to him. Magpie's face was haggard and drawn, the dark rings beneath his eyes betraying several long, sleepless nights. In his arms he held a rough piece of stone. Jacobs had half a mind to snatch it from Magpie and run the cart's wheels over it.

This wasn't how things were supposed to be, he lamented to himself. Jacobs and Magpie had been a team since childhood, stealing milk bottles from doorsteps and conning beggars out of their pennies. No job was too small for them, no profit too meagre. As adults, they had gone into the rag-and-bone business together, but were always willing to try their hand at something else – street hawking, sewer cleaning, prisoner transportation. . .

Which was how their troubles had begun, Jacobs thought dolefully to himself. When Magpie had stolen that wretched stone from the boy at the gates of the Bedlam, at first Jacobs had been amused. Served the little bleeder right for such crazy talk: the Crimson Stone, indeed! But when Magpie turned up for work the next day still clutching the rock, the joke began to wear a little thin – and disappeared entirely when he stopped talking to his partner.

To make matters worse, Magpie's obsession meant Jacobs had to work twice as hard to earn a living. Already that morning he had sold a large bundle of linen (being careful to under-change the nearsighted washerwoman), and a set of silver candlesticks that, whilst not actually silver, were close enough to avoid feeling any guilt about pretending otherwise.

There was a low snore by his side. Magpie had passed out in the cart. Great – now Jacobs would have to handle the rest of the day's negotiations on his own.

He didn't cheer up until the cart creaked into Dwindling

Road and a dilapidated building loomed into view. To most Darksiders, it was known as the Wayward Orphanage; for the young Jacobs, it had been home. It had been within the Wayward's walls that he had first met Magpie, where he had learned his first lessons in the vital subjects of cheating, conning and stealing. Every time he passed it, a wave of teary nostalgia always overcame him. Briefly, Jacobs thought about nudging Magpie awake, then decided against it.

Outside the front of the orphanage, he saw a bath chair – a light, hooded carriage favoured by the borough's more genteel inhabitants – resting at the side of the pavement. The rest of the street was deserted. Jacobs' nostrils began to itch with the opportunity for a quick profit. Bringing his cart to a halt, he licked his palm and smoothed down his straggling hair, then strutted over to the bath chair.

"G'd afternoon, m'lud or lady," Jacobs began, with a sweeping bow. "And what a fine afternoon it is, too."

At the sound of his voice, the figure shrank back into the sheltered darkness of the bath chair. There was no reply.

"I can't help but notice that you are outside the world-famous Wayward Orphanage," Jacobs continued, undeterred. "If you would like a guided tour, please allow me to offer my 'umble services. I am proud to admit that I was once one of the orphanage's charges, along with my good partner Magpie. See?" Fishing around his dirty vest, he pulled out a metal token with a number etched next to the initials "W.O." "Number 439: that was me. Magpie's got one too."

"I don't need a guide," the voice replied, in a barely

audible tone. "I know the Orphanage all too well, though it has been many years since I last saw it. Old memories, recently stirred."

Jacobs hadn't the foggiest idea what the stranger was going on about. He or she didn't sound quite right in the head. What was it with everyone these days? Rather desperately, he gestured beyond the slumbering form of Magpie at the junk heaped on his cart.

"Then perhaps I could interest you in some of our high-quality wares. We can meet your every desire: finest lace, priceless antiques, rare curios. . ."

Jacobs flashed his lone tooth in what he hoped was an enticing smile.

"No, thank you. I don't—" There was a sharp intake of breath from inside the bath chair. "What's that your partner's carrying?"

"That thing?" Jacobs said, surprised. "We nicked it from some crazy little blighter who claimed it was the Crimson Stone. Right little joker, 'e was."

"It's very . . . interesting," the voice whispered. "Could I buy it?"

"Ah." Jacobs scratched his head. "You see, we might have a problem there. Technically, this 'ere brick is Magpie's, and as you can see, he is not quite with it at present. There's no way I could sell it without talking to him first."

"I'll give you fifty pounds for it."

"Done," Jacobs replied instantly.

Unwilling to trust Magpie's compliance in his current mood,

Jacobs crept up into the cart and gently prised the stone from his partner's grasp. Magpie murmured, but didn't stir. With the stealth of a cat burglar, Jacobs climbed down and tiptoed back to the bath chair. A pair of slender hands reached out from the darkness and exchanged the stone for a wad of notes, the buyer careful to keep his or her face in shadow. Barely able to believe his luck, Jacobs was back in his cart and urging his nag on before the stranger could even bid him farewell.

As he rattled home, the rag-and-bone man whistled a jaunty air, all his cares forgotten. Magpie never tired of telling Jacobs that he was no thinker. Who was going to look foolish now?

Their current home was a barge moored on the bank of the Darkside Canal. It sat low in the turgid black waters, perpetually threatening to sink to the bottom. Decades of dirt and rust had long since obscured the name painted on its side.

At the sound of the approaching cart, a shaggy terrier raced out of the cabin to greet them, barking enthusiastically. Miraculously, considering the squalor, its white coat was clean and free of fleas, its stomach well fed. Jacobs clambered down from the cart and boarded the boat, crouching to ruffle the dog's ears.

"Hello, Tinker," he said. "I hope you've been a good dog today and haven't made any more messes. Uncle Jacobs hasn't got another pair of shoes to spare, you little rascal."

As the dog yapped happily in response, Magpie stirred in the cart. Suddenly aware that the stone was no longer in his arms, he looked about him frantically. As Jacobs gave him a happy wave, he got down from the front seat and stomped aboard the boat.

"You ignore Uncle Magpie," Jacobs wheezed into the dog's ear. "He's in a right mood today, and no mistake. But I've made everything better, just you see."

Tinker frowned at the approaching Magpie, and padded away.

"Good kip?" Jacobs called out brightly.

"Where's the Stone?" his partner replied blankly.

"You'll never guess what I did with it." Jacobs' face broke into a beaming smile. "I sold it."

"You did what?"

"I sold it! To some head case in the street. And look what the duffer paid for it!" Jacobs pulled out a wad of notes from his vest and waved them about excitedly. "Fifty notes, my old friend. You wouldn't believe it, if they weren't all here before your eyes. 'Ere – what are you looking at me like that for?"

There was a dark look in Magpie's eyes.

"You sold the Stone," he repeated dully.

"For fifty pounds! And it was for the best, Magpie! That thing was making you right funny in the head. You'll thank me in the end, I tell yer."

Magpie didn't look very grateful. As he took an ominous pace towards him, Jacobs backed away across the narrow deck of the barge.

"Listen here – seeing as you were the one what took it in the first place, you can have forty pounds," Jacobs bartered, somewhat desperately. "I'll keep ten, on account of me selling it. Fair's fair."

He held out the money with a tentative hand. Without even glancing at it, Magpie swatted the notes from his hand. Jacobs gasped in horror as the money fluttered over the side of the boat, finding a soggy grave in the murky waters of the canal.

"Are you off your bleedin' nut?" he screamed. "We could have lived off that for years!"

Magpie wasn't listening. As he advanced, Tinker came scampering in between the two men, taking up a protective position in front of Jacobs' ankles. He barked angrily at Magpie, who aimed a vicious kick in the dog's direction. Yelping with fear, Tinker scurried back to the safety of the cabin.

Jacobs retreated down the side of the canal boat, making frantic pacifying gestures with his hands.

"It was just a stone, Magpie!" he sobbed. "A harmless brick!"

With a snarl Magpie launched himself at Jacobs, who toppled backwards into the canal. Water closed in over his head like soup – spluttering, he felt ten strong fingers close around his throat. Jacobs reached out in a desperate attempt to break free, only succeeding in ripping Magpie's Wayward Orphanage token from the chain around his neck. The last thing Jacobs ever saw, through the grimy waters, was the face of his oldest friend, murder in his eyes.

*

Samuel Northwich cried out in his sleep.

It felt like his brain was on fire. He clutched at his temples, screaming with agony. Visions of the Crimson Stone flashed through his mind. Even with it no longer in his grasp, he could still feel its rough edges in his hands, its intoxicating control over his mind. At that moment, moaning pitifully, Sam knew that the Stone had been taken somewhere far away.

His stay in the Bedlam had been one of unending horror. Numb with shock at the Stone's sudden removal from his grasp, he barely remembered the journey from the front entrance: a blur of staircases, pleading cries from behind cell doors, the deathly cold touch of the warden as it pushed him onwards. Eventually Sam had been stopped outside an open door and flung headlong into the cell beyond. The door was slammed shut behind him with the finality of a coffin lid.

When his eyes had finally acclimatized to the darkness, he found himself in a sparse cell, with no furniture save for a cot and a coarse blanket, and a metal pail to relieve himself in. The window had been bricked up. Sam was utterly alone. The atmosphere of the asylum warded off the most basic of creatures – despite the cell's unsanitary conditions, no insects scuttled up the bare walls or crept across the floor.

Sam would have been glad for any sort of company. He had been scared of the dark since he'd been a baby, and the horrors his mind imagined lay in wait for him there. Now he was alone, his fears grew until he scrambled into bed and hid underneath the blanket, his whole body shaking.

With the Crimson Stone gone and no one to talk to, Sam tried to lose himself in daydreams. But no matter how hard he tried to imagine himself in sunlit meadows and busy, cheerful streets, he could never escape from the screams and gleeful, insane cackles that echoed around the Bedlam. Some of the inmates imitated birdcalls, others the hollering of monkeys. At times, Sam felt an urge to join in with them, to abandon himself to madness. Only the thoughts of the Stone kept him going. If he was going to escape and reclaim it, Sam knew that he had to stay sane. No matter how far away the Stone had been taken, he'd get it back eventually.

"Hello?"

At the sound of the woman's voice, Sam nearly fell out of bed with shock.

"Who's that?" he called out fearfully.

"I'm in the next cell," the woman replied, her calm, lilting voice washing over Sam like a cool mountain stream. "I heard you cry out. What's wrong?"

"It's my stone," Sam said, his voice drenched with misery. "Someone's taken it out of Darkside. I felt its pain as it crossed the boundary."

"Oh," the woman said. "I take it this stone was important to you?"

"It meant everything, miss."

A sigh drifted through the wall. "Believe me when I say I know how you feel. I lost some very important things when I was put in here. But I haven't given up hope of seeing them again, and so neither should you. What's your name?"

"Sam, miss." The boy sniffed. "I'm scared."

"Well, don't you worry, Sam," the woman said kindly. "I've been here a lot longer than you, and I've survived. We can keep each other company. Look down by the floor."

There was a soft scraping noise, and then a pale, slender hand appeared through a hole in the brickwork like a ghost. Tumbling out of bed, Sam took hold of the hand and squeezed it tight. He prayed that it would never let him go.

"What's your name, miss?" asked Sam.

There was a pause.

"Miss?" Sam whimpered. "Are you all right?"

"Yes," the lady replied faintly. "I'm fine. It's just that it's been so long since I spoke to anyone that I've almost forgotten my name. But you can call me Theresa, Sam. Theresa Starling."

10

Even given the wintry dawn outside, the atmosphere inside Vendetta's townhouse was a chilly one. If Jonathan had been hoping that Carnegie's rescue would put him in a good mood, then he was to be sorely disappointed. The wereman paced up and down the morning room, muttering curses under his breath.

Stifling a yawn, Jonathan wondered if he was ever going to get to bed. It had taken them all night to come back from Bleakmoor, carefully skirting the busier parts of the borough. Outside an abandoned cotton factory, Jonathan had reluctantly said farewell to his Night Mare. The horse gave him a final searching glance before tossing its yellow mane and cantering away over the cobblestones. They walked the remaining distance, keeping to the shadows lest a Bow Street Runner should appear.

They had returned to find the rest of the group waiting for them: Raquella and Alain leafing through Vendetta's books while Marianne and Harry played cards. There was no sign of the vampire, enabling a happy reunion to take place.

"Did you have any problems finding the others?" Jonathan asked Raquella.

The maid shook her head. "They were hidden in a dip close to the wood. In the chaos, it wasn't difficult slipping away."

"Last I saw, the hunters were still chasing after Lucien's horse," laughed Marianne. "They're probably still out there now."

"That was a pretty impressive distraction," Jonathan said. "How did you know Carnegie was going to go through the wood?"

The bounty hunter favoured Jonathan with a sparkling smile. "I didn't *know*. But that place was the only cover for miles around. If you keep going across open ground, then the horses will catch up with you in seconds. It's what I would have done, anyway. It would seem we think alike, Carnegie."

The wereman sniffed, unimpressed. "Wouldn't be so sure about that," he rumbled.

Carnegie was restless and irritable, his mood only darkening when he learned the fate of Theresa Starling. He glanced at Alain but said nothing. Then he began to pace.

"Now I've got two reasons to kill Lucien," he muttered. "Don't usually need more than one."

"Lucien can wait," said Jonathan. "My mum can't. We have to get her out of the Bedlam."

Raquella put down her book and caught Jonathan's arm.

"Are you sure you want to do this?" she asked softly. "Your mum has been locked in the Bedlam for over a decade. You don't know what that would do to a person, Jonathan. She might not be the woman you and Alain remember."

"She's right," Marianne added, unexpectedly. "This is a dark place you're going to, and there's no telling what you might find in there."

"I don't care what's happened to her," Jonathan said defiantly. "She's still my mum, and I'm getting her out of there whether you help me or not. If I have to, I'll do it on my own."

The bounty hunter gave Alain an arch look. "Awfully determined when he gets going, isn't he?"

"You have no idea," Jonathan's father replied meaningfully.

"This is all well and good," Carnegie cut in, "but it isn't going to get us into the Bedlam. We can't just knock on the gates and ask to see Theresa. The place is built like a fortress, and we aren't much of an army."

"It can't be that hard," said Harry. "People don't usually try to break *into* asylums. Usually, it's the other way round."

Carnegie smacked his hand into his palm. "That may be the most useful thing you've ever said, Pierce. If we want to find out how to get into the Bedlam, there's only one man to ask."

"You don't mean Sickheart, do you?" Marianne asked. Noting the inquisitive looks in the room, the bounty hunter explained: "Florian Sickheart is a painter who lives down in the Nook. Years ago the *Informer* ran a story that he had escaped from the Bedlam in his youth. Sounded like a load of hogwash to me, even if Sickheart is crazy enough to have been committed. You know what artists are like."

"Well, it's worth the trip," Carnegie rumbled. "The boy and I will go and ask him a couple of questions." He looked up sharply. "Where d'you think you're going, Pierce?"

Harry froze halfway up from his seat. "I thought you might want a hand."

"You sit tight and finish your card game," the wereman said curtly. "I'm the detective round here – me and the boy will be more than enough. Lucien's going to be combing Darkside for us, and the fewer of us out on the streets, the better."

Setting his stovepipe hat firmly on his head, Carnegie marched out of the room without another word. Shrugging at his friends, Jonathan made to follow. It seemed he wasn't going to sleep after all.

Jonathan waited until they were safely in the back of a hansom cab before venturing to break the silence. Carnegie was staring moodily out of the window, watching the houses flash past. The pavements were jammed with Darksiders, who had gathered in shocked huddles around posters proclaiming Lucien's new conspiracy tax. Voices rang out in disbelief as they tried to digest the news; scuffles erupted as some tried to tear down the posters, only to be stopped in their tracks by the brutal intervention of the Bow Street Runners.

Word of the Night Hunt spread through the packed crowds like smallpox or cholera, on the backs of urchins' whispers and the tittle-tattle of fishwives. Cowed by the watchful Runners, most Darksiders were careful not to show their pleasure at the Ripper's humiliation – but not every bitter laugh was stifled.

"What's Lucien up to?" wondered Jonathan. "At this rate the whole borough's going to want to kill him."

"They can get in the queue," Carnegie replied darkly.

"Is everything all right?" Jonathan asked the wereman tentatively. "You seem a bit . . . narked."

Carnegie harrumphed, not looking away from the window. "I'm over the moon, boy. Just not sure about this merry gang you've put together. Marianne may be handy in a scrap, but I trust that woman about as far as I can throw her. And as for Vendetta. . ."

"I know it's strange," Jonathan replied. "But we can't take on Lucien on our own. If Marianne or Vendetta can help us, we've got to accept it."

"Perhaps. But mark my words, boy, this is going to end

badly. I can feel it in my bones."

The wereman didn't speak again until they had reached their destination – an alleyway running down between two derelict houses. When Carnegie instructed the cab driver to wait for them, the man simply laughed and drove off.

Looking into the dark opening, Jonathan drew his coat around him. "Doesn't look very welcoming down there."

"This is the Nook, boy. What were you expecting, balloons? Come on."

Jonathan hurried after the wereman as he trudged along the snowy alleyway. The roofs closed in above their heads, the last light of the winter afternoon fading as the sky disappeared from view. During his time in Darkside, Jonathan had witnessed poverty and deprivation. But the Nook was something else. A frantic confusion of blind alleys and intersections, it was a world of permanent night. One overcrowded dwelling followed another, their smashed windows staunched with rags and cardboard in the vain hope of keeping out the wind. Some of the houses weren't even made from brick, but were flimsy lean-tos composed of scavenged wooden planks. Above their heads, washing hung limply from poles thrust out into the air.

Everywhere Jonathan looked, he saw the signs of illness – corpses of dead animals in the streets, the foul overspill from blocked sewers, and packs of feral children clad in rags. The children stopped as he and Carnegie went past, eyes as wide as saucers, staring at Jonathan as though he were an alien. Some cupped their hands together in a plea for money; others tugged beseechingly at his sleeve. For the price of a copper coin, one lucky child was chosen to lead them to Florian Sickheart.

The artist lived in a garret beneath the eaves of a decrepit building in the depths of the Nook. Carnegie and Jonathan walked through the open door and hauled themselves up the wooden staircase, past a quarrelling family whose raised voices threatened to bring down the building around their ears.

Florian Sickheart's garret was a monument to deprivation. The floorboards were blackened, the furniture battered, and the walls streaked with grime and filth. A painting was hanging above the empty hearth, a complicated whirlpool of black lines. The artist himself was standing by an easel in the corner of the room. At the sound of Carnegie's footsteps, he turned around. A deep scar ran like a canyon down Sickheart's face, from the peak of his forehead to his jawbone. His right eye was shut, while his left darted manically around in its socket. Wild ginger hair shot out in all manner of angles. Despite the freezing cold, he was shirtless and barefoot.

"You're not Maude," he said, cryptically.

"No," Carnegie agreed. "But I'm sure she'll be along later. In the meantime, maybe you'll talk to us."

From the moment they had entered the garret, Jonathan had had the uncanny sensation that he was being watched. As he looked up, he jumped. A single giant eye had been painted on the ceiling, a dark circle that looked down over the room. There was a malevolent depth to the pupil that made Jonathan shudder. When Florian lay in his bed, the eye would have dominated his vision: the last thing he saw at night, and the first thing in the morning.

"Beautiful, isn't it?" Sickheart said wistfully, following his eye up to the ceiling. "I have tried to capture it so many times, but never like this. It is the curse of the artist, you know."

"Very striking," Carnegie said, in a conversational tone. "But we didn't come here to talk to you about art. We wanted to ask you about the Bedlam."

Sickheart froze, then returned to contemplating the blank canvas on his easel.

"Rumour has it that you spent some time in there," the wereman continued. "And that you escaped from it."

Sickheart shook his head vigorously. "Nobody escapes from the Bedlam," he said.

"Not what I heard. Heard that you did."

The artist tugged at his hair in distress. "This isn't right," he moaned, gesturing at the easel. "I have a painting to finish, but now you come here and disturb me with all these *questions*!" Grabbing Carnegie by the lapels of his jacket, Sickheart shook him violently. "I must be left alone to create, do you understand?"

The wereman nodded, carefully prising Sickheart's fingers from his clothing. "Of course I understand. And the sooner you talk to us, the sooner the questions will stop and you can get back to your masterpiece. Also," Carnegie added in a whisper, "I hear it's harder to paint when all your fingers are broken."

Sickheart blanched. "Barbarian! You wouldn't dare!"

"Try me."

The artist slumped down on to the floor, defeated.

"It wasn't my fault," he began sorrowfully. "I was the victim of a cruel misunderstanding. My parents were crude peasants, with no comprehension of the many forms of genius. They thought I was. . ." Sickheart tapped the side of his head, as though unable to say the word "mad".

"I can't imagine why," Carnegie said drily.

"Indeed, indeed!" Sickheart squeaked. "I tried to make them see sense, but they wouldn't listen. They carted me off like a common criminal and threw me in a cell. With the voices." The artist clutched at his legs and rocked slowly back and forth. "No matter how I tried to shut them out, the voices wouldn't leave me alone. In the end, I couldn't take it any more. I decided I would escape, or die in the attempt. Thankfully, the voices came to my rescue. They told me which way to go."

"But if you managed to escape, why didn't they try to lock you up again?" Jonathan asked.

"Didn't you hear what I said?" Sickheart shouted, taking Jonathan by surprise. "Nobody escapes from the Bedlam! If I was outside it, then – ergo – I never could have been *inside* it." He relaxed, apparently calm again. "Elementary, really, when you think about it."

It didn't seem elementary to Jonathan. In fact, it

sounded insane.

"But why do you care?" Sickheart asked curiously.

"We need to get inside the Bedlam," Jonathan replied. "We want you to tell us how."

A look of horror dawned on Sickheart's face. "Inside? But why? The voices – you can't escape them, you know. They leave their mark on you."

"We'll take our chances," Carnegie replied firmly. "How do we get in, Sickheart?"

The artist pointed at the canvas hanging on the wall behind him. "Take it," he said quietly. "I have no use for it any more."

Carnegie frowned, looking at the lines swirling across the canvas. "What use is a painting to us?"

"It's not a painting, silly," Sickheart tittered. "It's a map."

"A map of what?"

Sickheart masked his mouth with the flat of his palm and pointed down through the floorboards.

"The sewers," he hissed. "The underground. That's how I got out, you see – tiptoeing through the tunnels. That's how. . ."

Trailing a finger across the scar on his face, he broke off with a whimper, his eyes wide from the memory. Carnegie strode over to the canvas and took it down from the wall.

"Thanks for this," he growled, clapping a hand on the artist's shoulder. "We make it out alive again, I'll bring it back to you."

"Alive?" Sickheart giggled like a child. "No fear of that,

silly. You're as dead as dead can be."

They left the artist sitting on the floor of his garret, rocking back and forth and giggling to himself. As Jonathan headed back down the stairs, the giggles turned to sobs, and the cries of Florian Sickheart dogged them all the way out to the street outside.

11

The Ripper's carriage rattled south through Darkside in a blur of gold and black, its lanterns burning fiercely in the early-evening gloom. Again and again the driver lashed his horses, until blood ran down their flanks and their mouths were flecked with foam. Traffic splintered at the sight of the ornate carriage and its unmistakable crest, cab drivers and tradesmen preferring to ride up on to the pavement or crash into street lamps rather than impede their ruler's progress.

Inside the carriage, a man with a gross paunch and a thick black hedgerow of a beard was ingratiatingly wringing his hands.

"My lord, it is an honour that you bless me with your confidence," he fawned at the man sitting opposite him.

"Yes, it is," Lucien replied bluntly. The Ripper was looking thoughtfully out of the window, his chin resting upon his right-hand knuckles. The streets were quiet, and those who hurried along the pavements did so with heavy shoulders. Whereas in the past, the encroaching night would have sent a ripple of gleeful anticipation through the borough, now the atmosphere was heavy with sullen fear.

"I would never have presumed to imagine that you even knew the name of Jeremiah Thunderer," the paunchy man continued, "let alone that you would give a mere preacher the honour of sharing your private carriage."

"Don't crawl," snapped Lucien. "I didn't bring you here to flatter me."

"No, sir. I am just surprised. I would have thought you would have preferred to discuss matters with Holborn. After all, he—"

"I don't care what the Abettor thinks," interrupted Lucien. "I rule Darkside, not him."

"Naturally, my lord, but his counsel is worth heeding. As everyone knows, Holborn's only concern is for Darkside."

"Holborn's concerns begin and end with how he can steal my throne. That's all you need to know."

Jeremiah's eyes widened. "You suspect the Abettor of treachery?"

"Suspect?" The Ripper laughed mockingly. "I see it in his eyes every time he looks at me. I hear it in his voice every time he opens his mouth. He would kill me without a second thought, if he could."

"But if you know that Holborn is plotting against you, why don't you take steps to stop him?"

Lucien waved a dismissive hand. "Let him scheme. The Runners obey my word and my word alone – his time will come. All my life I have been planning for this moment. I have fought and killed for it. I am hardly going to let Aurelius Holborn take it away from me now."

There was a commotion up ahead at the side of the road. A Bow Street Runner erupted out of the side of a ramshackle house, a bag of coins jangling in his giant hand. A gaunt man raced out after him through the door, a brood of young children around his legs.

"Please don't take that," he implored the Runner. "It's all we've got!"

The Runner ignored him, walking on to the next dwelling. As the Ripper's carriage rattled past him, the man recognized the livery, picked up a stone and hurled it at the vehicle. The Runner turned around and picked up the man by the throat, hauling him away even as the children pleaded with him for mercy. Lucien smiled thinly.

"It appears that there is some discontent among my loyal citizens. Why do you think that is?"

"It is not my place to guess the whims of the common man, my lord," the preacher replied cautiously.

"I asked you a question," said Lucien. "I expect an answer."

Jeremiah hesitated. "It is the new tax, my lord," he said carefully. "As it is, the poorer of your citizens struggle to gather enough pennies to buy food. If they have to pay your tax, they face starvation."

Lucien shrugged. "There's always another option," he said. "They can leave."

"Leave? And go where?"

"Tell me, preacher: do you think the world begins and ends at Darkside's boundaries?"

"Lightside, my lord?"

Lucien leaned forward. "Why do you think I have levied this tax? Do you think I covet the coppers of paupers? Holborn is a short-sighted fool – all he can think about is ruling the borough. I have other plans in mind for Darkside."

Jeremiah raised a bushy eyebrow. "Which are, my lord?"

"Bring it into the light."

The preacher gasped. "But . . . I don't understand!"

"I don't expect you to." The Ripper ran a hand through his cropped dark hair. "How could you? No one understands this borough better than me. I *am* Darkside – reviled as a murderous cripple, ostracized by my 'betters'. For over a hundred years, this borough has been a dirty secret, ignored by the rest of London. And we have been content to meekly hide ourselves away. Not any more – I will squeeze Darksiders out of this borough one by one, until nobody can ignore us. We are too strong, too powerful, to spend our lives skulking in the shadows."

The carriage had left behind the narrow, strangled streets of central Darkside, and was now careering along the broad approach to Devil's Wharf. In the distance, huge steamship funnels formed a haphazard silhouette on the horizon. The preacher delicately cleared his throat.

"And what, if I may ask, is my role in this?"

"I want you to spread the word. You, Jeremiah, will be my voice to the people – to Darksiders and Lightsiders alike."

The portly preacher respectfully inclined his head. "I am at the Ripper's service, my lord."

"Good. I thought you might say something like that." Lucien banged on the ceiling of the carriage, which slowed to a halt. The Ripper leaned across Jeremiah and pushed open his door. "Now, I have business to attend to – an unsavoury affair that a man like yourself would not want to witness."

"You want me to get out here?" Bewildered, Jeremiah looked around the wharf. Drunks were stumbling out of the nearest tavern, slurring as they berated one another, while knots of burly sailors loitered menacingly in the shadows. "This is hardly the sort of place for a man of my stature to be frequenting. There are all sorts of unscrupulous characters here!"

"Then I wouldn't linger, if I were you," the Ripper replied curtly. "Now get out of my carriage."

Thunderer stepped hesitantly down on to the wharf. Lucien watched with amusement as the portly preacher staggered off into the gloom, his hands clinging to his valuables. Then the Ripper banged on the carriage ceiling.

"Onwards!" he shouted.

Below decks of the SS *Blackbeard*, Alberto della Rosa sat quavering in the engine hold, his legs drawn up against his chest. His brow was bathed in sweat, and there was a hunted look in his eyes. Around him engines trembled and needles flickered across dials. But the ship wasn't moving. For the hundredth time that day, Alberto checked his pocket watch. The *Blackbeard* was supposed to have left port an hour ago. Alberto had no idea where the ship was bound for, and he didn't care. The only thing that mattered was getting out of Darkside.

He had been on the run since early morning. Word had got out that the Bow Street Runners were arresting members of the Night Hunt as punishment for the event's dismal failure, and the della Rosas had quickly moved to smuggle Alberto out of the borough. He had been transported down to the docks at the bottom of a crate of fruit, and was brought aboard the *Blackbeard* as the captain was presented with a weighty bundle of pound notes. Alberto's riding gear had been tied up in a bundle and burned, while his hat – lovingly adorned with bloodstained feathers from an eagle Alberto himself had butchered – now lay at the bottom of the harbour. Every trace of his involvement in the Night Hunt had been destroyed. All that remained now was for this accursed ship to move!

There was a loud creak above his head, and then the door to the engine hold opened. Alberto froze. He watched with horror through the gaps in the rungs as two feet descended slowly into the hold, each step ringing on the metal like a death knell. At the bottom of the steps, a man turned and hobbled into the light.

"Lucien!" Alberto gasped.

The Ripper nodded slowly.

"B-But," stammered Alberto, "h-how on earth did you find me?"

"The captain recognized you. Despite your handsome bribe, he thought better of aiding someone fleeing from the Ripper. He's been holding the ship for my arrival."

Alberto choked back a sob of fear. "I wasn't fleeing from you, my lord. My family merely thought that I was looking ill, and that a trip on the sea would be good for me. The sea air, you understand."

"I do understand," replied Lucien. "That's why you're hiding in the hold. Enjoying the sea air."

"I'm still honoured that you came to see me. I know how busy you are."

"Well, you know what they say," the Ripper said, with a cold smile. "All work and no play makes Jack a dull boy."

"I know that you are angry about what happened on the Night Hunt, but truly it wasn't my fault!"

"You were in the wood on Bleakmoor."

"And I had the boy trapped, my lord! But the wereman jumped me from behind. There was nothing I could do!"

"You let them escape," Lucien said sharply. "And now two of my greatest enemies are free to run around the borough, stirring up trouble. I blame you for this."

"Please forgive me. If you give me another chance, I will track them myself. I swear it!"

"The Bow Street Runners are seeing to that. I hardly require your services."

Alberto shifted fearfully. "So why are you here?"

"I think you know why. I can't have people letting me down. I need my subjects to know that there are consequences for those who fail me. Deadly consequences."

"But I'm from the one of the wealthiest families in Darkside!" Alberto wailed, scrambling back against an engine as Lucien hobbled towards him. "You can't do this to me!"

"I can do anything I want to you. I have power at my disposal of which you can only dream. Although, for you, it will be less of a dream, more a darkest nightmare. Be grateful that the Black Phoenix will ensure it ends quickly."

Lucien threw back his head, emitting an inhuman screech, and the hold was instantly submerged into inky darkness. There came the sound of giant flapping wings, and a set of razor-sharp talons came arrowing out of the unnatural night. Alberto screamed.

12

They waited until the middle of the night before daring to slip out through the front door of Vendetta's townhouse, six hooded figures hastening through fog-bound streets: Jonathan, Carnegie, Marianne, Harry, Raquella and Alain. The wereman had argued against so many people travelling to the Bedlam, but no one wanted to be left behind. As Alain quietly pointed out, with everyone committing to overthrowing Lucien, now was hardly the time to deny anyone a role.

Having spent hours deciphering Sickheart's map, they had decided that the best place to enter the sewers was on a side street running off the Grand. They walked swiftly through the borough, grateful for the fog's protection. Jonathan's insides were churning with excitement at the possibility of seeing his mum again. By contrast, Alain Starling was tight-lipped, his face drawn. It was almost as though Jonathan's dad was scared of hoping that Theresa might actually be alive.

Through the fog, Jonathan saw Marianne crouch down by an iron grille in the gutter by the side of the pavement. As the rest of the group took shelter in a doorway, he ran to help the bounty hunter lift up the sewer cover. As they moved the grille to one side, a stench rose up from the tunnels below like steam from a bubbling cauldron. Even given the rancid atmosphere that hung over Darkside like a cloud, the smell possessed a pungent foulness.

Marianne wrinkled her nose. "Charming," she murmured.

A ladder led down from the sewer entrance to the tunnel floor. Aware of the danger of lingering too long in the street, Jonathan took a deep breath of fresh air and then plunged into the sewer, clambering hand-over-hand down the ladder, the smell making his stomach recoil. On reaching the bottom of the ladder, he found himself standing in a dank tunnel with curving walls. A narrow walkway ran alongside the left-hand side of the tunnel, next to a dirty brown river. Water lapped gently against the brickwork. In the distance, he could hear the eager chittering of rats.

As they congregated on the walkway, Marianne produced a torch from her bag and carefully set it alight. Carnegie removed Sickheart's folded map from his pocket and studied it thoughtfully, his craggy skin a landscape of scars and pockmarks in the torchlight. Eventually the wereman looked up and nodded along the tunnel.

"This way. And keep your eyes peeled. I've heard some nasty stories about creatures lurking down here, and I've got a feeling they might be true."

Thinking back to Sickheart tracing the long scar that ran down his face, his eyes wide from some hidden memory, Jonathan could well believe it. He trailed after Carnegie, trying to ignore the sewer water splashing up over his shoes. Behind him, he could hear Raquella trying to bite back sounds of revulsion.

They crept through the labyrinth of sewers for what felt like hours, trusting the unsteady guiding hand of Florian Sickheart. Jonathan's mind was filled with images of the crazed artist splashing through the same tunnels, blindly fleeing from the Bedlam and the voices that haunted him. Shivering at the thought, Jonathan moved closer to Carnegie – nearly colliding into the back of him as the wereman came to an abrupt halt.

"What's going on?" asked Marianne, from the back of the group.

"Might be a problem," Carnegie replied.

Peering over the wereman's shoulder, Jonathan saw that the pathway sloped down into the water, disappearing beneath the surface. The tunnel continued beneath a low archway covered in brown lichen.

"Looks like we're going to get our feet wet," Carnegie called out over his shoulder.

"You've got to be kidding!" Harry retorted. "You want us to wade through that?"

"If Sickheart's map is right, then we haven't got any choice. It doesn't look too deep – we should be all right."

The wereman drew his long coat around him and

splashed down the slope into the water. Jonathan held back, reluctant to follow the wereman through the yawning archway and into the filthy darkness beyond. Then, remembering who might be waiting for him on the other side, he gritted his teeth and plunged into the sewer water. Though his nose had slowly become accustomed to the foul odour, the sensation of the cold, slimy water around his legs was still disgusting. He shuddered as something brushed against his legs. Jonathan couldn't see through the scum on the surface, which was probably a blessing in disguise.

They were swallowed up by the archway, disappearing into a dark so profound that Marianne's flaming torch barely made an impact. They waded in single file, the waterway deepening until the water lapped Jonathan's waist. He kept his chin up, determined to keep the water from splashing in his face, his mind trying to think of happy memories.

Jonathan jumped as something grabbed his arm. It was Raquella.

"What was that?" she whispered.

"What was what?"

The maid paused, looking warily from side to side. "I heard something."

"Probably just a rat."

"Sounded like a very big rat," Raquella replied, looking unconvinced.

To his immense relief, Jonathan saw a pinprick of light up ahead. Gradually the tunnel widened, coming out in a large underground cavern where three sewers came together to form a glassy black lake. At the far end of the cavern, a walkway had been built into the rock, and an iron ladder led up from it to the ceiling. Lanterns hung on the walls at even intervals.

"We're here," Carnegie exclaimed with satisfaction. "That ladder should take us up to the Bedlam."

"That's a shame," Harry said, his tone suggesting precisely the opposite. "I was really enjoying wading through all that—"

"Yes, thank you, Harry," Alain cut in testily. "Given that the end of this horror is in sight, do you think we could get a move on?"

He waded out of the tunnel and into the lake, Raquella and Carnegie close behind him. Although the surface was as still as a mirror, the water was deeper than before. Jonathan made slow progress, his feet feeling out foothold after foothold on the bottom.

He was halfway across the lake when something brushed against his leg. He froze.

"What is it?" Harry called out.

"There's something down here," Jonathan reported, through clenched teeth. "Something alive."

Marianne drew her sword.

"I felt something too," she said crisply. "There must be a shoal of fish down here."

They had all stopped now, watching the bounty hunter as she peered down through the water. Then Harry cried out, suddenly sinking from view. Before Jonathan could reach him, the boy came bouncing back up again, coughing and spluttering.

"What is it?" Marianne asked urgently.

Harry shook his head, hair plastered to his face.

"Something grabbed me! I managed to kick out but it's strong!"

"To the side!" roared Carnegie. "Move!"

Jonathan tried to run, but with the water high up around his neck, it was like crawling with lead weights attached to his feet. Frantically he scanned the surface for a sign of movement, but the still waters gave no clue to what lay beneath them. Carnegie had reached the side of the lake and was helping Alain and Raquella out when Marianne suddenly cried: "Jonathan! Look out!"

There was a roaring sound all around him, and then suddenly a giant red island rose up between Jonathan and the lake's edge. As the water cascaded from it, Jonathan made out a bulbous, conical head, with mottled flesh that was a deep, angry red colour. He found himself staring into the same giant eye that he'd seen painted on to Florian Sickheart's ceiling. Marianne had been wrong – there wasn't a shoal of fish in the pool, only one: a giant octopus.

Though every muscle in Jonathan's body was screaming at him to run, he remained rooted to the spot, mesmerized by the black, unblinking eye in front of him. The octopus's head was surrounded by a writhing mass of long tentacles, suction cups gleaming in the light. As a tentacle came whipping towards Jonathan, Harry charged across the pool and barged into his left side, sending him toppling into the water. The foul liquid closed in around his head, threatening to drown him. Flailing wildly, he burst up through the surface, only to see that one of the octopus's tentacles had wrapped itself around Harry and was hoisting the boy high into the air.

Jonathan ducked as another fiendish tentacle sliced over his head. Out of the corner of his eye, he saw Marianne toss him the flaming torch.

"Catch!"

Jonathan dived forward, clutching the torch handle before it fell into the water. He held up the flaming brand, waving it above his head in the hope of drawing the octopus's attention. The creature's skin had darkened with fury until it was almost black. As another tentacle coiled towards him, Jonathan jabbed the torch against its mottled skin. The creature flinched in pain, and with a cry Harry tumbled down from the air, hitting the water with a splash. Dropping the torch, Jonathan dived back beneath the surface and hauled the boy on to his feet.

"Come on!" he shouted.

As the two boys half stumbled, half swam for the shore, Jonathan heard Raquella shout out a warning. Glancing over his shoulder, he saw a tentacle spearing out after them like a malevolent snake. Just as Jonathan was about to dive back under the surface, the octopus made a piercing sound of distress and hastily withdrew its tentacles.

Friendly hands reached down from the lake's edge,

lifting Jonathan and Harry to safety. As he lay panting on the ground, Jonathan could see that one of the octopus's huge black eyes now had a dagger sticking out of it like a splinter. Marianne had remained in the shallows, her sword raised for a follow-up strike. As the octopus shrieked again and began to retreat, she took a threatening step after it.

"Marianne!" Carnegie roared. "Leave it!"

The bounty hunter stopped, giving the octopus a lingering glance as it sank back beneath the waves. Then, sheathing her sword, she turned and hauled herself out of the lake and up on to the pathway. Back on dry land, Marianne brushed at her clothes in disgust, trying to remove the sheen of filth.

"You want to leave that thing to get us on the way out?" she asked the wereman.

"I'd dance with the Ripper before going back through these blasted sewers again," Carnegie growled. "We'll find another way out. Everyone ready?"

Jonathan glanced at Harry, who shrugged. "I've got a feeling today's going to be one of those days. We might as well get on with it. After you, Carnegie."

The wereman grasped hold of the ladder and began climbing towards the Bedlam. As Jonathan followed suit, he took a final look back at the lake, its waters now as glacial and still as when they had entered, with no hint of the horror that lay beneath them.

13

The Bedlam was coated in taut silence: the sound of a thousand people holding their breath. As they crept along a dark corridor, with every step Jonathan expected an alarm to start ringing, or a guard to step out and challenge them, but no one did. It felt as though they were the only people in the entire world.

"Doesn't look like anyone's expecting us," Harry whispered.

"This one time," Carnegie growled softly, "I could do without a welcome party."

As they emerged from the corridor into the asylum's main hall, Jonathan gasped. The vast chamber was filled with a network of small platforms connected by interlocking staircases that ran off in different angles and directions. Here and there, cells had been built in seemingly random places: some on top of platforms; some beneath; others built into the walls themselves, somehow reached by stairways lying on their side in mid-air. The layout seemed to defy all logic, and in places, gravity. There was a tortuous magnificence about the architecture that made Jonathan feel both awed and afraid.

"Well, we're here," Marianne said briskly. "Now what? Start knocking on doors?"

Jonathan shrugged. "I guess."

Now that they had made it inside the asylum, he wasn't exactly sure what to do. One thing was clear – judging by the scale and the complexity of the Bedlam, checking all the cells was going to take a while.

Carnegie sniffed, and wiped his nose on his sleeve. "Well, one thing's for sure: we're not going to find anyone down here. Let's start looking, shall we?"

Keeping to the shadows by the asylum wall, the wereman led them up the nearest staircase, his footsteps echoing loudly in the hush. They came out on to a suspended stone platform, with staircases branching off from every edge.

"Which way now?" asked Harry. "Toss a coin?"

"What is going on here?" an imperious voice said.

As one, they whirled round, to be confronted by a small woman standing at the top of the stairs behind them. Dressed in a starched blouse with a buttoned collar and a long pleated skirt, she looked like a prim schoolmistress. Her hair was pulled into a severe bun, and a pair of small reading glasses rested on the bridge of her nose. In her left hand she carried a long cane.

"What is it to you?" Carnegie rumbled back.

"I am the Bel Dame," the woman replied. "This is my asylum."

Marianne stepped forward. "Pleasure to meet you, ma'am," she said, with an ingratiating smile. "We were just visiting a friend of ours. Perhaps you could tell us where she is?"

"No visitors are allowed in here," the Bel Dame said sharply. "I won't allow them. You must be inmates. What are you doing out of your cells?"

"No, we're not inmates," Marianne replied patiently. "We're not insane, you see."

"*Everyone* inside the Bedlam is insane. Those are the rules."

"Apart from you, I'm guessing," Carnegie growled.

The Bel Dame chuckled merrily. "Oh, quite the contrary. I am the maddest person here."

There was a certainty in her voice that left Jonathan in no doubt that she was telling the truth.

"It stands to reason," the Bel Dame continued. "How else could I control the wardens?"

The wereman frowned. "Wardens?"

A movement in the darkness above his head caught Jonathan's eye. As he looked up, the hairs on his neck rising in horror, he saw that the staircases above their heads were covered in creatures clinging to their undersides: spindly, man-sized beings whose skulls had been completely stripped of flesh.

"Look out!" he called. "They're all around us!"

Carnegie swore loudly, and Marianne drew her sword. They began to warily circle the platform, necks craned as they prepared for the wardens to drop down on to them.

The Bel Dame smiled thinly. "Now that you understand the situation, are you going to go back to your cells quietly, or are we going to have a disagreement?"

"I'm a fairly disagreeable man," growled Carnegie.

"Very well," the Bel Dame said briskly. "Don't say I didn't warn you." Then, brandishing her cane, she screamed at the wardens: "Get them!"

At her command, the Bedlam came alive, wardens swarming over the staircases towards them. They hunched over as they ran, talon-like fingers scraping the floor, skeletal faces glowing in the dark.

As Carnegie rolled up his sleeves and stalked over to meet them, Marianne grabbed Jonathan's arm.

"Get out of here," she said, pointing at the staircase running off to the left. "Take Alain and Raquella and go look for your mother. We'll make sure no one follows you."

"You can't take all of these things on by yourself!"

Marianne raised an eyebrow, tucking a curl of fluorescent blue hair behind her ear. "Oh, really?"

"Go on, Jonathan!" Harry urged.

With a final reluctant glance, Jonathan turned and ran up the staircase after Alain and Raquella, the first sounds of battle beginning behind him.

*

It was like walking through a nightmare.

They raced up one ghostly staircase after another, only to discover that the Bedlam didn't follow the normal rules of other buildings. Corridors branched off at crazy angles, only to end at a sheer brick wall. Flights of stairs had steps missing from the middle of them, making it impossible for anyone to continue upwards. Jonathan had a strange sensation that the building itself was mocking them. As they climbed, at intervals he could look down and see the silver arc of Marianne's sword as she battled the wardens. The bounty hunter had been true to her word – none of the creatures had come up after them.

The fighting had awoken the inmates of the Bedlam, who now erupted into a distressed chorus from behind their cell doors: barking and babbling; laughter so hard it must have hurt their lungs; and softer, futile whimpers and sniffles. Jonathan paused at every door, peering through the small spyglasses at the inmates beyond. Some scrabbled around on the floor like animals; some lay rigid on their cots, unable to move. Sometimes the noise was so bad that Jonathan couldn't bring himself to look through the spyglass, for fear that he might find himself staring at his mum.

That was the worst thing about this place. Theresa Starling had spent over a decade here. What would that do to a person? How could anyone hope to stay sane here? What if Raquella had been right all along – that it would be better for Jonathan if he didn't find his mum? Jonathan tried to shut the thought out from his mind.

He was glad that his dad was with him. Even though Alain was no Carnegie, Jonathan still took comfort from his presence, as if nothing bad could happen to him whilst Alain was there. Raquella followed a pace behind them, a pensive expression on her face.

After coming to a wider platform, Jonathan peered into what appeared to be an empty cell. Checking the shadowy corners for movement, he lingered at the spyglass while Alain and Raquella moved on to the next staircase. He was just about to move on when he heard someone whisper his name.

"Jonathan!"

The voice was high-pitched and mocking, like a child's playground taunt. He turned round, but there was no one in sight. He thought he must have imagined it.

"Jonathan's lost his mummy!" the voice continued. "Can anybody find her?"

"Who's there?" Jonathan called out.

"Nobody can find her, and we know why!" the sing-song voice went on.

Suddenly desperate to get off the platform, Jonathan broke into a run as he made for the staircase.

"*She's dead!*" the voice snarled after him.

Jonathan hared up the steps three at a time, nearly crashing into Alain and Raquella at the top of them.

"Are you all right, son?"

"Not really," Jonathan panted. "Can you hear voices?"

Alain nodded, a grim look on his face.

"What are they saying?"

"You don't want to know."

Raquella shivered, drawing her shawl closer around herself.

"I'm glad it's not just me," she said. "I didn't say anything because I was worried that *I* was going mad."

Alain patted her hand, and put an arm around his son's shoulders.

"Come on," he said softly, leading them on to the next staircase. "They're just voices. We'll ignore them together."

Harry had been fighting for several minutes before he realized that he was enjoying himself. Perhaps it shouldn't have been so surprising. After all, he was a Ripper, heir to a tainted bloodline that trickled down from Jack himself. But ever since his father's death, Harry had fought to suppress the thirst for violence that dwelled within his soul. Now, trapped within this crazed hellhole, he was free to unleash it. The very fact that his life was in the balance gave him a thrill, as though a deep need was being answered.

Initially, the three of them had fallen back, protecting the staircase up which Jonathan had fled. Urged on by the Bel Dame, the wardens rained down upon them, elbowing each other out of the way in their desire to kill. But if they thought that they had stumbled across easy prey, they quickly learned otherwise. Blessed with a preternatural speed and agility that even the wardens couldn't match, Harry dodged their flailing attacks, striking back when they were off-balance. Alongside him, Marianne and Carnegie displayed their contrasting fighting styles: the bounty hunter a study in deadly elegance, her sword swooping in and out of the darkness; the wereman all brute force, a raging maelstrom of teeth and fists. Though they fought in different ways, the results were the same – the staircases were now littered with the bodies of wardens. Undeterred by the carnage, wave after wave still came after them, razor-sharp nails reaching out longingly for flesh and eyeballs.

As one of the creatures darted towards him, Harry leapt up in the air, delivering a shuddering kick to the warden's skull that sent it flying over the edge of the staircase. With Jonathan safely out of sight, they had begun battling up through the Bedlam, navigating the treacherous flights. Fighting back-to-back with Marianne, Harry came out on to an exposed platform in the very centre of the hall. There was no protection at the edge – one misstep would send them plunging to their doom.

Overwhelmed by the beast within him, Carnegie was fighting in a blind rage. With a savage bellow, he picked up one of the wardens and hurled him towards the platform edge, not caring that it was straight in Harry's direction. The creature knocked into Harry just as the boy was about to leap into the air, catching him off-balance and sending him staggering backwards, until suddenly there was nothing beneath his feet and he was falling.

Harry flung out a desperate hand, his fingers latching on to the edge of the platform. He dangled in the air, the muscles in his arm burning with the strain of clinging on. The Bedlam stretched out below him, a dizzying drop to its floor.

"Finish off the boy!" screamed the Bel Dame.

A skeletal head loomed over the platform's edge above Harry. He was done for.

14

At that same moment, in the skies above Darkside the moon peered out from behind a veil of sooty clouds, casting a pale sheen of light over Pell Mell, the broad approach to Blackchapel. It illuminated a long, elevated passageway that ran across the borough's rooftops, linking one of the main towers of the palace with a set of luxurious private gardens a half a mile away.

For over a hundred years, the Ripper's Corridor had allowed the first family of Darkside to cross the borough without having to endure the stench of the sewers, muddy their feet in puddles, or sully themselves with the stares of their subjects. Since its construction during the early years of Jack's reign, only a handful of people had ever had the privilege of using it. Now a lone figure was striding down the tiled hallway.

Aurelius Holborn pulled the hood of his cloak up over his head, cursing the moon. Drenched in its light, his outline would be visible through the corridor's windows to anyone happening to look up from the pavements of Pell Mell. Tonight, the last thing he wanted was to be seen. He had even forgone his customary armed escort, aware that the clank of weaponry and heavy tread of boots would draw attention to his journey. Whatever happened tonight, he was on his own.

In all the years that he had served Lucien's father, Thomas, effectively running the borough as the once-proud ruler withered into old age, Holborn had never before presumed to use the Ripper's Corridor – though he had had the foresight to make a copy of Thomas's keys. Had his mission been less urgent, the Abettor would have lit the dormant torches on the wall and inspected the hanging portraits, or lingered at the windows to enjoy a view of Darkside so few had seen. Instead he hurried along the passageway with barely a glance around him, before descending a steep flight of steps and unlocking the heavy iron door at the end.

The air hung crisp and cold above the tangled expanses of the gardens. Protected from view behind high stone walls, Holborn relaxed a little. Footsteps crunching in the snow, he kept to the path, mindful of the toxic caress of the belladonna and poison ivy in the flower beds. Stone plinths had been set into the earth – bases for the Bow Street Runners, they stood empty, waiting for the brick golems to return to the gardens. Here their skin would harden and they would revert to statues, untouched by the passage of years.

The path curved, revealing the tower that formed the garden's macabre centrepiece. Whereas the Rippers had their mausoleum – where their bodies would lie in ceremony for immortality – the remains of their enemies were condemned to this place, the Charnel House, carted in wheelbarrows by ghouls and tipped into the bone depository inside. For years the Rippers had come to this tower and gazed with satisfaction on the crumbling skeletons and dismembered corpses of those foolish enough to cross them.

Glancing around him to check that there was no one watching, Holborn hastened up the steps towards the Charnel House. The key turned in the lock with a clunk, and as the door opened, a draught of air steeped in decay assailed the Abettor. Ignoring the smell, he slipped inside the building and locked the door behind him.

Moonlight was seeping in through the grilled windows, bathing the Charnel House in a sea of white. Everywhere Holborn looked he saw bones: shelves groaning under the weight of skulls, pits overflowing with skeletal remains coated in a thick layer of dust and cobwebs. Thigh bones were scattered forlornly across the floor, while skeletal hands reached out almost imploringly at the Abettor, as though begging for a proper burial.

Holborn waited, shivering in the draughts. He had taken a risk coming here, he knew, but the message he had intercepted – meant for Lucien's ears alone – had spoken of a matter of utmost urgency. The Abettor was beginning to wonder whether he had made a mistake when the foundations of the Charnel House began to tremble, and Brick McNally erupted through the stone floor.

Despite the many occasions Holborn had seen the Bow Street Runners enter in this fashion, the sight still sent an awed thrill down his spine. McNally slowly scanned the vault, the bricks in his neck grating against one another as he looked around the tower.

"I sent word that I was to speak with the Ripper," he said finally, sending a cloud of soot spewing into the air. "Where is he?"

"Otherwise engaged," Holborn replied curtly. "One of the Night Hunters made the mistake of trying to leave the borough. A decision I imagine they're regretting, if they're still alive. Until Lucien returns, you can report to me."

The Runner stood motionless, an inscrutable expression on his rocky face. There was something about McNally that set him apart from the rest of the golems – an ability to calculate that Holborn distrusted as much as he respected it. Eventually McNally nodded and continued.

"We have made progress. Today we tracked down two of Marianne's henchmen – the ones known as Humble and Skeet."

Holborn smiled, his teeth glinting in the darkness. "Excellent, McNally. Where did you find them?"

"They were hiding out in a public house down at Devil's Wharf. A drunk steamer captain fell foul of them in a brawl, and informed us of their whereabouts as revenge."

"Did they come quietly?"

"There was a brief struggle," McNally replied, a dismissive note in his voice. "A host of Runners are transporting the prisoners back to Blackchapel as we speak."

"Have they given us any clues as to Marianne's whereabouts?"

"They say they haven't seen her since Lucien's succession. We'll see whether a spell in the cells changes their minds."

Holborn picked up a skull and gazed at it thoughtfully. "And the mood on the streets?" he asked casually.

"Fear, mostly," McNally replied. "And anger."

"Anger?"

"The new Ripper has not endeared himself to the people. His tax hits the pockets of those who can least afford it. Already the cells beneath Blackchapel are filling up with non-payers. There have been slogans scrawled on walls; rumours of plots and conspiracies building against him."

Holborn was glad that the moon had disappeared behind a cloud, so that darkness obscured the gleeful expression on his face. Lucien's plummeting popularity only increased the chances for revolt. And if Holborn were to manoeuvre himself to the head of the people, who would be better placed to assume the throne?

"The Runners serve the will of the Ripper," McNally continued, "but the Blood Succession is over. We should be back here in the garden where we belong, not on the streets. We are not tax collectors."

"Perhaps," Holborn replied delicately. "But you know as well as I do that the Runners can be called upon in times of great danger. It is clear that there is a powerful conspiracy against Lucien. You must stay until it is defeated."

McNally shrugged, sending a powerful ripple across his brick shoulders. "Even so. Thomas Ripper would not have disturbed us for this. Neither would any of his predecessors."

"Thomas Ripper is dead," Holborn shot back, tossing the skull back on to the pile. "Just another pile of dusty bones and withering skin. Lucien sits upon the throne, and you *will* do his bidding."

The Runner inclined his head. "As he orders."

"Is that it, McNally? I was informed that you had vital information to bring before the Ripper."

"There is one more thing."

"What? Tell me and I shall pass it on to Lucien."

McNally dived back beneath the surface of the floor before exploding upwards again, the eruption sending a human figure flying into the air. The man crashed face down on to the flagstones with a sickening thud. Holborn flipped the man over with his foot and inspected his face. The Abettor grimaced. Doused in a heavy musk of body odour and alcohol, the man was bruised and unshaven, his clothes little more than rags.

Holborn wrinkled his nose with distaste. "Why have you brought this . . . *thing* here?"

132

McNally inclined his head towards the unkempt man. "We found him wandering around on the edge of the borough. He was trying to cross over to Lightside."

"And?" The Abettor's voice struck an imperious note. "I can't be expected to take an interest in every vagrant and down-and-out you pull off the streets."

"He says he was following the Crimson Stone."

"The Crimson Stone?" Holborn chuckled sonorously. "The fellow's unhinged!"

"He is – but that doesn't mean he's wrong. Just like the Crimson Stone, the Runners are made from Darkside's bricks and mortar. We share a kinship with it. The Stone was taken across to Lightside several hours ago – I felt it myself."

Holborn leaned forward. "The Stone exists? I had always thought it a myth!"

"It is all too real," said McNally. "The Stone is both part of Darkside's fabric and its master – it can reduce the mightiest of buildings to a heap of pebbles in the blink of an eye."

"And how the devil was this man hoping to find it in Lightside?"

"Once the Stone has touched your mind, it will never let you go. He will be able to track it."

"Let me get this clear," Holborn said slowly. "Are you telling me that this man can lead me straight to the Crimson Stone?"

"It can lead Lucien," McNally corrected. "The Stone belongs to the Ripper, and him alone."

"Of course, of course," Holborn said soothingly,

inwardly cursing his slip. "But as I said, Lucien is currently indisposed. I don't want to disturb him until I can be sure that we can trust the guidance of this tramp."

The man stirred at Holborn's feet, looking up with filmy, bloodshot eyes.

"Where's the Stone?" he mumbled. "It's mine – give it back to me."

"What's your name, my friend?" the Abettor asked, adopting a friendly manner.

"Magpie," the man slurred back.

"Well, Magpie, I don't have the Stone. But I can help you look for it. Can you walk?"

Still dazed from his subterranean transportation, the man didn't reply. Holborn slowly helped Magpie to his feet, trying not to breathe in his fetid stench. He brushed down the man's tattered clothes in a kindly gesture.

"Are you intending to cross tonight?" McNally asked.

"There is no time to waste," replied the Abettor. "If the Stone fell into the wrong hands, there is no telling the threat that could pose to Lucien. As you said, McNally, the mood on the streets is turning ugly."

The Runner extended a stone arm towards a trapdoor set into the floor of the Charnel House.

"The quickest way is through there."

"There is a crossing point right here?" Holborn breathed.

McNally nodded. "The first Ripper created it himself, tapping into the power of the Crimson Stone. Jack used to travel back to Lightside this way when he wished to . . . amuse himself. Over the years, it has fallen into disuse."

Holborn couldn't believe his luck. It was as though some dark gods were smiling upon him. The Abettor lifted up the trapdoor and then, slipping a supporting arm beneath Magpie, half pulled, half carried the stunned tramp towards the hatch. As the mismatched pair disappeared down through the opening, Brick McNally watched them leave, his face an impassive wall.

15

As the warden looked down at Harry, the faintest hint of a smile ghosted across the creature's face. With a deliberate slowness, it placed its foot on the boy's hand and began to push. Harry gritted his teeth, aware of the sound of his knuckles cracking. It was all he could do to hang on.

There was an ear-splitting roar, and suddenly the warden went flying past Harry towards the asylum floor. As the boy felt his grip faltering, a shaggy hand reached down and grabbed his shirt, hauling him back up on to the platform. Harry found himself face to face with Carnegie – the private detective's face covered in a hairy, feral mask.

"Thanks," Harry panted. "That was a close one."

There was no sign of recognition in the wereman's eyes, only malevolent craving. Fearful that Carnegie might attack him, Harry tensed. The wereman barked dismissively, then turned and loped away across the platform, diving headlong into a melee of wardens.

As he caught his breath, Harry inspected his wounded hand. It was covered in an ugly purple bruise, but it didn't appear to be broken. To his right, Marianne buried a punch in a warden's stomach, then ran the creature through on her sword. She strode over to Harry.

"You all right?" she asked crisply. Her blue hair was flecked with blood – as far as Harry could tell, none of it hers. He nodded.

"Then back to it, nephew," she said, gesturing at another wave of wardens charging up the staircase. "We're far from finished yet."

Elsewhere in the Bedlam – it could have been far away, or just around the corner – Jonathan was giving up hope of ever finding his mum. The search was taking for ever, and given the rambling architecture of the asylum, there was no way to be sure which cells they had checked. It was a struggle not to be overwhelmed by the sheer desolation of the place, and the voices running through their heads. The whispers were unceasing, pricking like a needle at Jonathan's deepest and most private insecurities. Under their influence, warm childhood memories suddenly twisted, the loving faces of his parents morphing into sneers.

Jonathan wasn't the only one suffering. They were halfway up a staircase when Raquella suddenly cried out.

"What is it?"

A distressed look crossed the maid's face. "It's the

voices. They said. . ." She trailed off. "I don't want to talk about it."

Now Raquella had disappeared around the corner with Alain, leaving Jonathan standing alone on a platform, in front of two side-by-side cells. He almost didn't have the heart to check them.

You'll never find her. She never loved you – neither does your father. . .

"Shut up!" Jonathan shouted. "Leave me alone!"

"Hello?"

Someone had spoken from behind the cell door, only this time there was no mockery in the voice, and even though Jonathan hadn't heard the soft Irish lilt since he was a toddler, there wasn't a single doubt in his soul who it could be.

"Mum?" said Jonathan, in a very small voice.

His heart sinking, Harry realized that the battle was turning against them.

Although man for man, the wardens were no match for Carnegie, Marianne and Harry, the sheer weight of numbers and their seemingly inexhaustible stamina was beginning to tell. Taking up a position at the back of her men, the Bel Dame waved her cane and screamed exhortations at the wardens, spittle spraying from her mouth.

Harry had battled his way to the highest level of the asylum, leaping over breaks in the staircases as the wardens spread up the walls like a plague. Now he,

Carnegie and Marianne were fighting at close quarters along a cramped corridor, wave upon wave of wardens funnelling after them. Harry could feel his muscles beginning to ache, and his reflexes dulling. A clumsy low blow from one of the wardens nearly caught him; at this rate, it wouldn't be long before one did.

"Nephew!" shouted Marianne above the din. "Above you!"

Harry glanced up to see a skylight above his head, its glass coated in years of grime and neglect. He leapt up towards the ceiling and smashed open the skylight, sending a rush of icy cold air pouring into the Bedlam. Grabbing hold of the ledge, Harry pulled himself through the skylight and on to the moonlit roof.

He rolled to one side, his breath coming in ragged bursts as first Marianne flipped up through the skylight, and then Carnegie did. The wereman had barely climbed to his feet before the wardens came swarming after them like a horde of ants.

Harry backed away towards the edge of the roof. The sloping tiles were coated in snow, making the footing doubly treacherous. As he traded blows with one of the wardens, Harry slipped to the floor. Narrowly avoiding a stamping foot, he kicked out, catching his assailant in the midriff. The warden fell to the ground, clutching its stomach.

Scrambling to his feet, Harry saw Carnegie still thumping away at his opponents; the wereman was showing no signs of tiredness. Marianne had been forced back to the roof's edge, her toes balanced on the guttering. Busy fending off a pair of wardens, she hadn't noticed the small figure creeping up behind her back.

"Marianne!" shouted Harry. "Behind you!"

The bounty hunter turned in time to see the Bel Dame rushing towards her, cane raised high in the air. Shifting her weight, Marianne dropped her shoulder, using the woman's momentum to flip her over. As the Bel Dame's scream turned from one of triumph to one of despair, the asylum mistress went tumbling over the edge of the Bedlam, and hurtled down towards a painful end on the cobblestones below.

Harry had been prepared for another frenzied onslaught, so he was amazed to see the fighting come to a sudden halt. With their mistress gone, the wardens appeared to lose all direction. They milled about on the roof, unsure what to do next. As Carnegie, Marianne and Harry walked wearily past them and climbed back down through the skylight, they barely seemed to notice. The last Harry saw of them, the wardens had crowded by the spot where the Bel Dame had fallen, and were peering mournfully over the edge.

It seemed impossible.

Even though this was the very reason they had entered the Bedlam, now that he had heard Theresa's voice, Jonathan couldn't believe it.

He was dimly aware that Raquella was by his side.

"What is it? Have you found her?"

Jonathan nodded numbly.

Taking a pin out from her flowing red hair, Raquella got down on her knees and slipped it in the lock. Jonathan gave her a startled look.

"I've been watching Harry," she explained, pressing her ear to the door as she jiggled the pin in the lock. "It seems like a handy skill to have."

There was a loud click, and the maid gave a small sound of satisfaction. She stood up and moved out of Jonathan's way.

"Take care in there," she said softly.

Jonathan nodded, and then slowly opened the cell door and walked inside.

The room beyond was a small, dark prison all of its own. A figure was hiding in the depths of the shadows against the far wall of the cell. Suddenly nervous, Jonathan lingered in the doorway.

"Hi," he said finally. "Are you OK?"

"I'm all right," the woman replied, in a faltering voice. "Who are you?"

"I'm Jonathan," he said.

Theresa's eyes widened. "Not . . . my Jonathan? Jonathan Starling?"

Unable to speak, his eyes brimming with tears, Jonathan nodded. The woman stepped forward, and for all the paleness of her skin and frailness of her frame, there was no doubt that this was the woman he had seen in his father's photograph, the woman who had cradled him as a child.

"Oh, my boy," said Theresa Starling. "You found me! It's been so long. . ."

She held out her arms, and suddenly Jonathan was hugging her, tears running down his cheeks. He wasn't sure how long they stood there. All he knew was that he didn't want the hug to end for a very long time.

There was a noise behind them, and Jonathan turned to see that his dad was standing in the doorway. With a choked sob, Alain stumbled into his wife's cell and enfolded her in his arms, shaking with emotion. Jonathan tried to move away, to allow his parents the moment alone, but Theresa's arm was clamped around him like a vice, and he too was folded into the hug.

It was at that moment, in the unhappy, permanent night of the Bedlam, that the Starling family was finally reunited.

16

Moving very slowly, Jonathan and his parents walked out of Theresa's cell, their hands clasped tightly together. Raquella was waiting in the corridor, the maid's face brightening into a cautious smile at the sight of them.

"Is everything OK?" she asked.

"It is now," Jonathan replied, glancing at his mum.

Hearing a noise at the top of the stairs behind them, Jonathan spun round and saw Elias Carnegie standing staring at them. The wereman's clothes bore the scars of battle, and there was a jagged cut down the side of his face, but the feral rage that overtook him in the heat of battle had drained away. Instead, there was a look of utter bewilderment on his face.

"I don't believe it," Carnegie muttered to himself.

Theresa chuckled softly. "Hello, Elias," she said. "It's been a while."

The wereman stood rooted to the spot at the top of the stairs, his eyes wide with disbelief. It was Theresa who walked slowly forward, kissed him on the cheek and slipped her frail arms around him. Carnegie patted her – awkwardly but gently – on the arm with a hairy hand.

"I tried to find you," he rumbled.

"I know," Theresa murmured back. "It's all right. Everything's all right now."

Alain stepped forward, and coughed politely. "Shall we go? I don't think we want to spend a second longer in this place than we have to."

The wereman nodded. "I agree. Harry and Marianne have gone looking for a way out that doesn't involve sewers and octopuses."

"Where are the wardens?" asked Jonathan.

"We had a run-in with the mistress of the asylum," Carnegie replied. "She made the mistake of picking a fight with Marianne, and paid the price for it. The wardens sort of lost interest after that. Doesn't mean we should hang around, though."

They were turning to walk away when Theresa suddenly cried out. "Wait!" she said, her hand flying up to her mouth. "I nearly forgot. Sam!"

Alain frowned. "Who?"

Theresa pointed back at the closed cell door next to hers. "There's a little boy next to me. We can't leave him here!"

Seeing the look in Theresa's eyes, Carnegie nodded. Raquella hurried back to the cell door and slid her hairpin inside the lock. Within a minute the door was open, and she was peering inside the cell.

The maid gasped. "*Sam?*"

Jonathan blinked with surprise. The last time he had seen Samuel Northwich, the boy had been a bright young magician's assistant. That had been barely six months ago. Now Sam was huddled in the corner of the cell, his face smeared with dirt. There was a haunted look in his eyes that spoke of an ageless, nameless pain.

At the sound of his name, Sam flinched and hugged his legs.

"Don't you remember me, Sam?" Raquella whispered softly, stepping into the cell. "It's Raquella. We were friends."

Sam whimpered, shrinking back even further into the darkness.

"There, there," Raquella said soothingly, slowly outstretching her hand. "I'm not going to hurt you. Take my hand and we can get out of this nasty place. Don't you want to get out of here?"

Sam nodded.

"Come, then. Take my hand."

The boy glanced around the cell, and then bolted towards Raquella. The maid hugged him, quietly making low comforting noises.

"Right," Carnegie barked. "Now it's time to go."

They headed down through the maze of staircases towards the ground floor, footsteps reverberating around the tortured architecture as the Bedlam silently mourned its dead mistress. It was with great relief that Jonathan realized that they had reached the asylum's entrance hall, and saw Marianne leaning against the open doorway. The bounty hunter took deep breaths of the freezing air as it swept inside the Bedlam.

"My nephew's gone looking for some transport," she reported, wordlessly acknowledging the increased size of their party. "He should be along any minute now."

Outside, the grounds of the Bedlam were coated in a thick covering of clammy fog. There was a whinny in the gloom, and then a carriage crunched along the driveway and drew up outside the front of the asylum. Harry was in the driving seat, wrestling with the reins.

"Where did you get this?" Jonathan asked incredulously.

"Borrowed it," Harry replied crisply. "Now get in before anyone starts asking any questions."

Jonathan hurried across the snow and opened the cab door, gesturing to his companions to enter the carriage. As they filed out of the Bedlam, Carnegie swung up to the driver's seat and took the reins from Harry's hands.

"I'll drive," he growled.

"Probably for the best," said Harry. "It's harder than it looks."

After the carriage was crammed with passengers, the wereman geed up the horses. As the cab pulled away, Theresa Starling took a final look back at the asylum as it disappeared into the fog. She swallowed, tears forming in her eyes. Alain squeezed her hand.

"Don't worry," he whispered softly. "It's over now."

They returned to Vendetta's townhouse before the sun came up, leaving the stolen carriage in a nearby side alley before dashing across the street towards safety. As they ran across the cobblestones, Sam slipped and fell to the ground with a cry. Carnegie reached down and picked up the boy, shaking his head as he carried Sam up the steps.

"I'm turning into a bloody governess," he muttered, to no one in particular.

Carnegie hauled Sam up to one of the bedrooms and laid the boy down on the bed. Raquella pressed her hand against the boy's forehead.

"He's burning up with fever," she reported.

"What do you think happened to him?" Jonathan whispered. "He seemed fine the last time we saw him, and now. . ."

The maid watched solemnly as Sam's eyes closed, and he fell muttering into a disturbed sleep.

"I've no idea," she replied. "But whatever it was, it struck to the very core of his soul."

They sat down to a cold breakfast in the drawing room, a reflective mood descending upon the gathering. Every now and then Jonathan found himself glancing at his mum, worried that she was going to disappear again. In daylight, he could see more of the toll that the Bedlam had taken on Theresa. Her hair had turned a startling shade of white, and her painfully thin frame bore testament to a decade-long diet of asylum food.

His mum wasn't the only person Jonathan was worried about. Despite the joyous wonder in Alain's eyes, Jonathan saw the beads of sweat glistening on his forehead. He knew that Darkside's fetid atmosphere was taking its toll on his father. Looking at both of his parents, Jonathan suddenly came to a decision. He was about to speak up when the townhouse door clicked open, and Vendetta slipped into the drawing room.

The vampire was dressed in an immaculate three-piece suit, a heavy cowled cloak resting over one arm and a copy of the *Darkside Informer* in his other hand. He tossed the cloak down on to a divan, exposing a large pink smear on the hem: a combination of snow and blood.

"Good meal?" Carnegie barked.

Vendetta drew the back of his hand across his mouth. "It sufficed. Though I am accustomed to a rather higher standard of cuisine."

"We had an interesting morning as well," Carnegie remarked in a conversational tone. "We went to the Bedlam. You should have come with us. It was fun."

If he was expecting a reaction from the vampire, he didn't get one. Instead Vendetta cast a cool eye over the breakfast table, noting Theresa Starling for the first time.

"You?" Vendetta arched an eyebrow. "I presumed Lucien had killed you off years ago. All in all, you're a remarkably difficult family to dispose of." He smiled. "Like cockroaches."

"Leave her alone," said Jonathan, through clenched teeth.

Theresa touched his arm lightly. "It's all right, son."

She turned back to Vendetta. "I remember you too. Vendetta the banker. I see you haven't changed much, even if your circumstances do appear somewhat reduced. I hope Holborn is taking good care of the Heights in your absence."

Anger flashed across the vampire's face, but he swiftly regained his composure. "He can have it for now," he said, with an elegant shrug. "The Abettor cannot remain so strong for ever, and the passage of time has little effect on the undead." He passed a critical eye over Theresa's frail frame. "Though I can hardly say the same of you."

"You vile—" Alain began, starting out of his chair.

"Please, Alain!" Theresa said, restraining her husband. "You've fought enough battles for one day. His words don't concern me."

"Well,. I'm delighted to hear that you can bear my hospitality. Should my generosity become too much for you, feel free to leave." Vendetta paused. "Though I fear your son may find the streets of Darkside a rather more perilous place than before."

"What do you mean?" Carnegie barked.

"Whilst I was on the streets I noticed a commotion taking place involving a newspaper boy. It appears that the new management of the *Informer* decided to put out a special edition. I took the liberty of purchasing a copy, and it made for interesting reading."

Vendetta unfolded his copy of the *Informer* and tossed it down on the table in front of Jonathan.

"Your notoriety is spreading," the vampire said, with elegant malice.

As Jonathan smoothed down the yellowed, crackling pages of the newspaper, he saw that the front page was dominated by a drawing of a young man that looked remarkably like him. His heart sinking, he began to read the accompanying story.

"The Only Informer You Can Trust"

THE DARKSIDE INFORMER

8th December, DY119

LIGHTSIDE PLOTTERS UNMASKED

Secret documents discovered in the desk of the disgraced former editor of the *Informer*, Arthur Blake, have revealed a foul plot aimed at the very heart of Darkside: Lucien Ripper. This conspiracy, concocted in the despised halls of power in Lightside, involves an attempt to pass off an imposter as the Ripper's slain sister, Marianne. Though such an attempt to deceive Darksiders would usually be considered laughable, the unprecedented scale of the conspiracy demands decisive action. Already the plotters have been stirring up trouble on the streets, leading more gullible citizens into extremely unwise protests against the Ripper's vital conspiracy tax.

On hearing the *Informer*'s warning of this grave threat to Darkside, Lucien Ripper immediately took bold steps, ordering the Bow Street Runners to remain on the streets to protect the populace. A ten o'clock curfew has been introduced, and will remain in place until the plotters have been rounded up. Anyone caught on the streets between the hours of ten and six o'clock in the morning will be adjudged to be part of the Lightside conspiracy, and will be dealt with accordingly.

The ringleader of this vile plot is thought to be a young man named Jonathan Starling (pictured inset). Any information leading to his capture will be rewarded with £500, the production of his corpse with double that. The *Informer* exhorts its readers to remain watchful in these dangerous times, and to help extinguish this dire threat to the borough.

Carnegie whistled over Jonathan's shoulder. "Five hundred pounds? You know that's a small fortune here, don't you?"

"If anyone sees you out on the street, you're done for," Harry added. "I've half a mind to turn you in myself."

The wereman gave Jonathan a searching look. "You don't seem that concerned, boy."

Jonathan pushed the newspaper away. "I'm not. It doesn't matter now, anyway. I'm leaving Darkside today, and I'm not coming back."

17

A shocked silence descended upon the drawing room.

"You're doing what?" Carnegie growled.

"I'm taking Mum and Dad back to Lightside," said Jonathan steadfastly. "And I'm staying there."

"What about Darkside?" the wereman shot back. "We may have got Theresa back, but it's not over, boy. Lucien's still on the throne. He was the one responsible for putting your mum in the Bedlam in the first place, or have you forgotten that?"

Jonathan looked down. "Of course I haven't forgotten that. And I don't want to leave things like this. But we have to go."

"So that's it?"

"Really, Carnegie, *do* stop being so tiresome."

As one they turned and looked towards the window seat, where Marianne was sitting with her feet up, staring out over the snowy street. The bounty hunter hadn't spoken for hours – Jonathan had almost forgotten she was there.

"This doesn't concern you, Ripper," the wereman snarled.

Marianne fixed Carnegie with a cold stare. "Believe me, I'd much prefer not to have to listen to your endless tiffs, but someone's got to point out the obvious. Jonathan doesn't want to leave our merry gang, but, unlike you, he's noticed that his father can't cope here."

"Now wait a minute—" protested Alain.

"Please, spare me the heroics," Marianne said, with a weary gesture of her hand. "You can't hide pain from me. I see every wince, every bead of sweat on your forehead. You spend much longer here, you're going to end up like that boy upstairs." She turned to the wereman. "Alain has to go back to Lightside, Carnegie, and of course Theresa and Jonathan are going with him. They've been apart for a decade – are you really going to begrudge them that?"

"It's not the time to be packing up and going home," Carnegie growled.

"Don't you see?" Marianne stretched languidly in the window seat. "This isn't about Jonathan any more, wolfman – or any of the Starlings, for that matter. This is about my brother and the fate of this borough. This is war."

"And which side are you fighting on?"

"Ours."

"We're going to fight side by side?"

"We did all right in the Bedlam, didn't we?" said Marianne.

Theresa smiled wanly. "As much as I'd like to help you

153

remove that beast from the throne, I'm not sure either I or Alain would be much use to you right now. Jonathan's right – our family should get out of Darkside."

"How are you going to cross back?" asked Raquella. "It's not easy at the best of times. With this bounty on Jonathan's head, it's going to be nearly impossible."

Vendetta glanced up from his newspaper. "I might be of some assistance there."

"You've got to be kidding," Jonathan said, with an incredulous laugh. "*You're* going to help us?"

"Starling, if it meant I'd never have to see your wretched family again, I'd carry you out of Darkside on my back. I have a carriage stabled at a secret location, and I can send word to one of my men, Yann. He'll bring the carriage here and take you back to Lightside."

"As easy as that?"

Vendetta shrugged. "You can make it more complicated if you wish."

Jonathan hesitated. The vampire was the last person he trusted, but one glance at his dad left him in no doubt that they were running out time. Reluctantly, he accepted Vendetta's offer.

Everything moved very quickly after that. Within half an hour, an unmarked carriage appeared outside the townhouse, the driver wrapped up in a thick overcoat and a low brimmed hat that covered his face. The Starlings said their goodbyes swiftly in the hallway, unwilling to draw them out. Vendetta remained upstairs, while Carnegie loitered uncomfortably at the back of the group, only softening when Theresa hugged him farewell. Then Jonathan's parents hurried out down the steps and into the waiting carriage.

Jonathan paused in the open doorway, suddenly reluctant to leave.

"Will you ever come back?" asked Raquella.

He looked back at the maid, then at his mum and dad inside the carriage.

"No," he said. "I don't think I can." He hugged Raquella quickly. "Good luck with everything. I'm sorry I have to go."

"Entirely understandable," Harry cut in, with a grin. "I'm just sorry you're going to miss out on all the fun."

"Fun? You're crazy." He took a deep breath. "Right. Time to go."

He was halfway down the steps when a voice called him back.

"Boy?"

Jonathan glanced back at Carnegie.

"Take care of yourself."

Before he could reply, the wereman walked away up the stairs. With a heavy heart, Jonathan turned his back on Carnegie and went to join his family in the carriage.

Night had fallen over Darkside, swathing Vendetta's townhouse in shadow. Its master had slipped out again, driven by the need to feed, while downstairs two Rippers and a wereman shared a restless, uncomfortable silence. On the first-floor landing Raquella glided along like a ghost, her flowing skirt rustling as it brushed against the wooden floor. She was long accustomed to darkened hallways: years of service at Vendetta Heights – where the blinds were kept closed and curtains drawn during daylight hours, lest a ray of sunlight fall upon her master's skin – had seen to that. No longer could phantom creaks on the staircase or the sudden chiming of clocks startle her.

Stopping outside Sam's bedroom, she gently pushed the door open and slipped inside. A gas lamp was burning dimly on the table by his bedside, casting a flickering orange glow over the boy as he lay curled up in a vulnerable ball in bed. He shifted uneasily in his sleep, mouthing words of distress.

Raquella picked up the gas lamp from the table and held it over Sam's gaunt face. Engrossed in examining the boy, she didn't hear the floorboard creak behind her.

"How is he?" a voice whispered into her ear.

Raquella nearly dropped the gas lamp in surprise, only for a hand to reach out and steady her. She whirled round, glaring furiously.

"For Ripper's sake, Harry!" she hissed. "Don't creep up on people like that!"

The young journalist looked wounded.

"I wasn't creeping," he protested. "I walk quietly, that's all."

Realizing that he was still holding her hand, Raquella snatched it away. "That *is* creeping, Harry."

"I was worried about waking the lad up," Harry said quietly, pointing at Sam. "Is he getting any better?"

There was a shadow of concern on his face as he asked. It was typical of Harry – one minute he was mocking her, the next he was trying to be nice. How could one boy be so frustrating?

Raquella glanced down at Sam.

"I don't know," she said truthfully. "Whatever ails him, it attacks his mind as much as his body. I doubt even a doctor could help him."

"He's been through something pretty dreadful, that's for sure."

"Perhaps the morning will bring an improvement," Raquella said. "Let's leave him to sleep."

They tiptoed back out on to the landing, the light from the gas lamp disappearing as Harry closed the bedroom door behind them. He caught Raquella's arm as she turned to walk away.

"I really didn't mean to scare you back there," he said. "I'm sorry if I did."

"I was surprised, not scared," Raquella retorted sharply. "You're the last person I'm scared of."

"Really?" There was a note of amusement in Harry's voice. "Not even a little bit? I am a Ripper, you know. We do have *something* of a reputation."

Raquella snorted. "Ripper indeed. You're nothing more than a conceited smart alec, Harry Pierce, and don't you ever forget it."

"With you around, I'm unlikely to," Harry replied ruefully. "You don't think very much of me, do you?"

There was a new note in his voice now – all traces of mockery had vanished. Raquella was suddenly aware of the closeness of his silhouette in the darkness.

"You're not all bad, I suppose," the maid said grudgingly. "There are moments when I don't find you completely irritating."

"Well, that's a relief," Harry said. Then he leaned forward and kissed Raquella softly on the lips.

She was too shocked to respond. It was only when Harry had pulled away that Raquella realized that her cheeks were burning, and her heart was beating rapidly in her chest. For once in her life, she had no idea what to say – or whether, in fact, she wanted to say anything at all.

The moment was shattered by a piercing scream ringing out from the bedroom.

Raquella ran back into the room to find Sam sitting bolt upright in bed, his face as white as a sheet.

"What is it, Sam? What's wrong?"

There was a wild look in the boy's eyes as he fended off the maid's attempts to comfort him. "It's the Stone!" he babbled. "I need the Stone back!"

"What stone?"

"The Crimson Stone!" Sam cried. "I took it! I took it and it was mine and then they took it away from me!"

"Who took it away from you, Sam?" came Harry's voice, from beside Raquella.

"The men in the night . . . the cart on the way to the Bedlam . . . a bird . . . thieving bird . . . Magpie . . . Magpie and Jacobs, their names were."

"And where are they now?"

"I don't know!" Sam howled. "They locked me up in the nasty place and took it away!"

The boy's eyes rolled up in his head and he slumped back on to the pillows, unconscious. As Raquella wiped his brow, the bedroom door flew open and Carnegie and Marianne burst into the room.

"Heard the scream," the wereman said gruffly. "Everything all right?"

"In a manner of speaking," replied Raquella. "I think we may have found out why Sam's ill. He was the one who took the Crimson Stone."

"Really?" Marianne leaned forward, her eyes glinting. "That little thing? How enterprising of him. And where is the Stone now?"

"Apparently two men took it from him," Harry said. "Do the names Magpie and Jacobs mean anything to you?"

"I've had the pleasure of their acquaintance," Carnegie said drily. "If this is true, Ripper knows what those two imbeciles have done with it."

"Only one way to find out," Marianne replied, with a dazzling smile.

18

Beneath a police station in Central London, Detective Horace Carmichael's world was falling apart.

The headquarters of Department D was a cramped underground room kept at arm's length from the rest of the station – rather like Darkside itself, Carmichael had often thought. At the height of summer, the room was as hot and breathless as a kiln; now, in the depths of winter, ice coated the pipes and dark patches of mould festered on the walls. Water dripped into a bucket jammed between two filing cabinets with maddening regularity.

Carmichael wasn't sure how many years he had been working down here. It was easy to lose track of time underground. Part of him didn't mind being out of the way. He knew that the other coppers on the force thought he was weird and didn't trust him. It wasn't just his hunchback, though Carmichael knew that it didn't help. He was just different. Even his superiors found some excuse to avoid eye contact, preferring to look down at their notes or gaze out of the window as they spoke to him.

The detective sat alone at his desk, surrounded by precarious tower blocks of files and paperwork. Behind him, a large map of London was pinned to the wall, its centre covered in a dark swirling stain like an inkblot: Darkside. Carmichael's eyes were glued to the battered portable television resting on top of one of the cabinets. On the screen, a news programme cut from one part of London to the other, reporters breathlessly gabbling into microphones. Across the rolling bar at the bottom of the screen, the headline ran: CAPITAL CHAOS.

"For any viewers just joining us," the female newsreader said, "we can report that London has today been witness to a series of inexplicable phenomena. A plague of rats has swept through Borough Market, feasting upon the fresh produce. The city centre is in a state of gridlock following a pile-up between a bus and a horse-drawn carriage on Tower Bridge. Meanwhile, officials at Tate Modern are refusing to comment on stories that an exhibition was disrupted by a large bull-headed creature rampaging through the gallery, goring hundreds of priceless works of art and several bystanders."

Carmichael glanced across at the telephone, which lay primed on his desk like an unexploded bomb. It was only a matter of time before the superintendent phoned. Any unusual stories – from blood-bank robberies to sightings of wild animals – were considered Department D territory.

Although Darkside itself was never mentioned, Carmichael's responsibilities were clear: to keep any overspill from the rotten borough a secret, and ensure that Lightsiders continued to be blissfully ignorant of the canker on their doorstep. In many ways, he was the perfect man for the job – after all, he was Darkside born and bred himself. Having endured a miserable childhood there, Carmichael had crossed over decades ago in the hope of starting a new life, only to find that there were even fewer opportunities for a hunchback in Lightside than in Darkside. A penniless and desperate Carmichael had drifted into a murky underworld, where criminals from both sides of London brushed shoulders with one another.

He was no natural criminal, and it was only a matter of time before he was caught. After a few months of petty thefts, it turned out that the fence Carmichael was using to pass off his stolen goods was none other than Silas Warriner – the founder of Department D. The undercover detective took pity on Carmichael, and gave him a choice: go to jail, or join his department. It didn't take the hunchback long to make up his mind.

Despite his unfamiliarity with police work, Carmichael quickly discovered that covering up the incursions from Darkside was relatively easy. Lightsiders accepted prosaic explanations for the most extraordinary of events, preferring to believe them the work of madmen or pranksters rather than face the darker truth.

Today's events, however, were a different matter. It was clear that an exodus had begun from Darkside, its inhabitants risking the crossing en masse. It was all Lucien's fault. The ridiculous conspiracy tax was bad enough; by ordering a night-time curfew on top, the Ripper appeared intent on making life in Darkside as unpleasant as possible. At this rate, the cells at Blackchapel were going to run out of room, and the trickle of crossers making for Lightside would become a flood.

Carmichael had already sent a strongly worded message of complaint to Lucien, but the Ripper hadn't bothered to respond. The detective was completely on his own. To his amazement, he had been told that Charlie Wilson had walked out of Department D, handing in a transfer request without even speaking to Carmichael. The hunchback wasn't sure how much worse things could get.

Back in the newsroom studio, the newsreader paused, and then said: "Now we can show you some mobile phone footage sent in by one of our viewers, who claims it shows the London Eye brought to a standstill by a giant swarm of bats."

As the screen was filled with a black, seething cloud, the telephone exploded into life. Sighing, the detective picked up the receiver.

The north-east corner of Hyde Park was quiet. Usually, this area – better known as Speakers' Corner – rang to the impassioned cries of the men and women who came to make public speeches, haranguing anyone who would listen. But today the sub-zero temperatures and the blanket of snow on the ground had persuaded most would-be orators to leave their placards at home, and their makeshift podiums of crates and stepladders resting in the garage.

However, not everyone had been deterred. In the middle of one of the broad thoroughfares that cut through the park, a small crowd had formed around a stage consisting of several planks bridging two oil drums. Without warning, the bronze braziers flanking the stage crackled into life, cutting through the winter gloom. A murmur of expectation rippled through the crowd.

A heavyset man with a large belly clambered up on to the stage, the planks buckling beneath his weight. He was dressed in a thick woollen overcoat buttoned stiffly up to his chin, while his face was framed by a thick beard and a resplendent top hat. The man came to a halt in the centre of the stage, imperiously surveying the sparse crowd. A snowball whizzed over his left shoulder. Ignoring it, the man held up his hands for silence.

"My name," he called out, in a voice as loud and clear as a trumpet, "is Jeremiah Thunderer. I stand before you today as a newcomer to your city. As a child, I had heard many tales of this place. As an adult, I dismissed them as fairy stories, bedtime make-believes." He shook his head sadly. "Only now do I realize that such tales told but a quarter of the truth. This place is indeed a haven for smug do-gooders, a sanctuary for self-righteous hypocrites."

The nervous titters that had greeted Thunderer's arrival had died away. He had the audience in the palm of his hand.

"I stand before you today," he repeated, his voice rising, "not only as newcomer to this city, but also as a messenger from the great Lucien Ripper. Over a hundred years ago now, you turned your backs on your brethren, your fellow city-dwellers, your neighbours and your streetmates, hiding them away in a dark corner like some shameful secret. Now the day of reckoning is upon you, Lightsiders, and my message to you is this: repent. Repent!" Thunderer screamed again, flecks of spittle flying from his mouth. "Or face the wrath of Darkside upon your souls!"

Back in the headquarters of Department D, Carmichael watched with a growing sense of resignation as the newsreader touched her earpiece, frowning, and then suddenly interrupted one of her guests.

"We're crossing live to the Tower of London, where our correspondent is standing by with some breaking news."

The camera cut to a red-faced man standing in front of the imposing castle. In the background, officers scurried back and forth behind a police cordon.

"Extraordinary scenes here," the reporter panted. "I can exclusively reveal that the Koh-i-Noor diamond – one of the most famous gems in the world, one of the most valuable in the royal collection, for many the crown jewel of the Crown Jewels – has been stolen! Details are only just beginning to filter through, but it is believed that a gang of four thieves somehow broke into the Tower last night, evading the guards, and made off with the diamond."

"This is astonishing," the newsreader said. "The security around the Crown Jewels is amongst the tightest in the world. How on earth did the thieves manage to bypass it?"

"A very good question, and one the police are trying to answer as we speak. Their job has been made more difficult by a very confused set of eyewitness reports. Apparently two figures were seen scaling up the side of the Tower with their bare hands – although that would appear to be an almost superhuman feat. There were reports of jets of flames in the night sky; one lady even claimed to me that she saw the thieves escape in a taxicab! At this early stage, the only thing we can say with any certainty is that these were no ordinary thieves."

The telephone on Carmichael's desk began ringing again. The detective groaned and put his head in his hands. For a minute he seriously considered not picking it up, but eventually he lifted up the receiver.

"Yes?"

It wasn't his superior. Carmichael listened carefully, a bemused expression on his face.

"The Crimson Stone? Yes, I know what it is. Who is this?"

After a pause, the voice told him. The detective's face went pale.

"You?" he breathed. "It can't be! It's been so many years. How on Darkside did you find me?"

As the voice began to explain, Carmichael sat back in his chair, a faint smile dawning upon his face.

"Incredible," he murmured. "All this time, and you've been right here. I'll come right now. Stay where you are."

Carmichael put down the phone and banged his fist on the table in celebration. Perhaps the day could be salvaged after all.

19

With the weather having brought the Darkside Canal's sluggish waters to an icy halt, a rowdy congregation of boatmen and lock keepers had gathered on its banks, warding off the cold with coarse stories, arguments and generous helpings of rum. One navvy was halfway through a particularly crude joke when he halted abruptly and stared at the two figures approaching them.

Women of any kind were a rare sight on Darkside Canal; well-dressed ladies, such as the one currently picking her way through the muddy slush on the towpath, a parasol protecting her from the snowflakes swirling in the air, were unheard of. Only a combination of sheer surprise at her presence – and the sizeable frame of the unkempt footman accompanying her – prevented the boatmen from deluging her with unwelcome offers of company. Instead they stared, open-mouthed, as the lady walked past them, politely bidding them good day. A couple of navvies even took off their hats.

It wasn't until the canal workers had been left far behind that the woman turned and hissed at her companion, in a most unladylike tone: "You're going to pay for making me dress up like this, wolfman."

"You're the one who insisted on coming with me, Marianne," Carnegie replied, in a low growl. "And with that bounty on your head, everyone in Darkside is going to be looking for you. At least dressed like this, no one's going to recognize you."

With her newly dyed orange hair pinned up beneath a small hat and a veil masking her distinctive pale skin, Marianne knew that the wereman was right. She wasn't entirely ready to concede victory, however.

"I insisted on coming with you because I had to make sure you didn't mess this up. If Magpie and Jacobs did take the Crimson Stone from Sam, then it's vital we retrieve it. It may be the only way we can take Blackchapel back from Lucien!"

"I've chased this stone before," Carnegie retorted. "More than likely this is a waste of time. Though given the fact that Lucien's beaten you once in combat, I can understand it if you're scared."

"Scared?" Marianne's voice was laced with acid. "I've never feared anything in my life. Don't forget that I've seen you fight my brother. If I recall, you were lying on the floor half-dead when I stepped in and saved your life. How long did it take for those wounds to heal?"

Carnegie didn't reply. They walked in fractious silence along the towpath until they came alongside a ramshackle barge that clung to the side of the bank by a frayed mooring rope. Carnegie nodded towards it.

"This is the boat we want." He bowed, with a wolfish grin. "My lady."

Casting the wereman a baleful glance, Marianne stepped gracefully aboard the barge, lifting up the hem of her dress to prevent it touching the filthy wooden decking. At the sound of her footsteps, a terrier raced out from the cabin and began bouncing around her ankles, yapping enthusiastically. The bounty hunter ignored it, brushing past the animal to explore the boat. It was Carnegie who got down on to his haunches and greeted the dog, a craggy smile dawning on his face.

"You're looking hungry, little guy," he muttered. "Someone not been feeding you?"

From the other side of the barge, Carnegie heard Marianne call out his name in an exasperated tone.

"Put the mutt down and come and look at this," she called out.

Reluctantly leaving the dog, Carnegie padded over to the stern of the boat, where Marianne was looking down on to the icy wastes of the canal. A battered shoe was sticking out of the frozen water like a small, dirty iceberg.

"I'm presuming there's a body on the other end of this," the bounty hunter mused.

"So why don't you pull it out and have a look?"

"What," said Marianne, gesturing at her outfit, "dressed like this?"

Muttering an oath, Carnegie reached over the edge of the boat and grasped the shoe. The wereman gritted his teeth and began to pull. There was a loud crack, and a body exploded from beneath the ice. Carnegie lifted it up and dumped it on to the deck with a thud. The corpse's face had turned grey and puffy, whilst his mouth had frozen open in an expression of shock, revealing a solitary tooth sticking out from his gums.

"Handsome devil," Marianne said wryly. "Recognize him?"

"That's Jacobs," Carnegie rumbled. "Looks like he had a falling out with someone."

"Magpie?"

The wereman shrugged. "Perhaps. But by all accounts, the two were as thick as thieves. Quite literally."

Marianne lifted up Jacobs' chin, revealing a set of bruises ringing the man's neck.

"Well, he didn't throttle himself. I've had a look around the barge – there's no Crimson Stone here, and there's no sign of Magpie."

"And finding him is another problem entirely." Carnegie paused. "What are you doing?"

The bounty hunter had stooped down and was fishing about in Jacobs' pockets.

"Searching for clues," she replied, with a grimace. "That's what detectives are supposed to do, isn't it?"

With a small sound of triumph, Marianne prised open Jacobs' fingers, freeing a circular token, the initials "W.O." etched into the battered metal next to the number 425. She held it up.

"This mean anything to you?"

Frowning, the wereman inspected the token. "I'm guessing it's some kind of identification tag – the 'W.O.' could be the Wayward Orphanage down in the Lower Fleet. Not sure what our friend Jacobs is doing with it, though. Perhaps he's paid the orphanage a visit recently. We should go and find out."

Marianne smiled brightly. "This private-detective business is easier than it looks, you know."

"Beginner's luck," Carnegie growled.

An hour later, they walked through the Wayward Orphanage's main entrance into a small courtyard dominated by a giant elm tree, its bare branches stripped by winter. Children ran and dodged around its trunk, screaming with excitement as they chased one another. At the sight of the newcomers, the children stopped as one and stared at them, their pinched faces betraying their inadequate diets.

"Don't mind us," Marianne said breezily, picking a path towards the archway on the other side of the courtyard. As Carnegie followed her beneath the elm tree, a child swung a hand down from the branches and snatched the stovepipe hat from his head.

"Hey!" the wereman snarled. "Give that back!"

Thumbing his nose at the wereman, the child scampered higher up into the tree. Carnegie grabbed the trunk and began shaking it fiercely, trying to dislodge the boy from his hiding place.

"For Ripper's sake, Carnegie," Marianne said, laughing. "Just go up there and get it."

Carnegie glared at her. "I'm a wereman, not a monkey."

"Oi! Robbins! I saw that!"

They turned to see an elderly man striding across the courtyard, his face blanketed in a thick grey beard and moustache. He was wearing a long scarlet coat with a sword strapped to his side, and moved with the clipped gait of a military man. He glared up into the tree.

"You return this gentleman's hat this second or I'll get the matron to give you a month's worth of ice-water bed baths. You hear me?"

There was a muttered expletive from amongst the branches, and then Carnegie's hat dropped to the floor like a giant black conker. The wereman brushed it down, still balefully eyeing the boy.

"Sorry about that," the man said briskly. "I'm Colonel Yardy. I run the orphanage."

"A pleasure to meet you," Marianne said sweetly. The Colonel went crimson, clumsily shaking her gloved hand. "A good job you intervened when you did."

"I should say," Carnegie said darkly. "The aptly-named Robbins was in for a short, sharp shock."

"Shall we go inside?" asked Yardy. "The children don't

get many visitors here, and the excitement tends to make the little blighters even more trouble than usual."

He led them through the archway and along a dank corridor to a large door covered in heavy locks and chains. After the Colonel had carried out a complicated unlocking process, he pushed open the door and led them into a cosy sitting room, where a fire was crackling merrily in the hearth and a fug of pipe smoke hung in the air. The walls were covered in sepia-tinted photographs.

"So then," he began, clapping his hands together. "What can I do for you?"

"I'm a private detective," Carnegie said. "Found this on a case I'm working on. Wondering if you could tell me anything about it."

He handed the Colonel the token, who took one glance at it and gave it back to him.

"This would belong to Magpie."

"Very impressive," said Marianne. "Can you do that with all the tokens?"

The Colonel smiled ruefully. "Only two, my dear. Number 425, Master Magpie. Number 439, Master Jacobs. Difficult to forget those scoundrels. Somewhere here there should be a photograph of them. . ." He glanced around the room, tapping his chin. "Now, where would it be? Aha!"

Seizing upon a photograph on the wall, Yardy took it down and showed it to Carnegie and Marianne. A group of Wayward children were pictured in the orphanage courtyard – the ground was covered in snow, and their thin linen dresses and bare legs offered little protection against the wind. The children looked freezing cold.

"That's Magpie there," Yardy said. "And his partner in crime."

A fresh-faced Jacobs and Magpie were loitering towards the back of the group, their faces wreathed with mischievous grins. They were a head taller than the other Wayward children, and the only ones smiling.

"As I said," the Colonel continued, "I am unlikely to forget those two. They were a pair of terrors from the cradle to the day they left here. One time, I remember, they were caught with a stolen polecat and a hundredweight of horse chestnuts—"

"Hang on a minute," Marianne said, a note of excitement in her voice. "Isn't that the Lightside policeman who keeps chasing after Jonathan?"

Carnegie peered at the photograph. Even though the photo was decades old, Horace Carmichael was instantly recognizable by the hunch on his back. He was standing apart from the other children, his face wary and old beyond its years. By his side stood a young girl, who was even smaller and more frail than he was.

"Ah, Horace," said Yardy. "Nice enough boy, but I can't pretend he was happy here. Children can be very cruel to one another. I've no idea what happened to him in the end. Some of us are just destined for an unhappy life, I fear."

"Carmichael's not the only familiar face here," Carnegie

growled, pointing at the young girl standing beside the hunchback. "Recognize her?"

Marianne let out a low whistle. "Unbelievable! She never said she knew Carmichael. What on Darkside is she up to?"

"I don't know," Carnegie replied darkly. "But I'll wager one thing: Jonathan's walked straight out of the frying pan and into the fire."

20

The Starlings' carriage had only just crossed back into Lightside when Alain let out a cry of anguish, and began twitching violently.

"Alain!" Theresa cried out. "What is it?"

"He's having a darkening," Jonathan replied. "The crossing's been too much for him." He banged on the roof of the carriage. "St Christopher's Hospital," he called out. "And fast!"

A whip cracked in response, and the carriage surged forward. As Jonathan wrestled with his father's flailing limbs, Alain babbled incomprehensibly, a frenzied look in his eyes. Spittle foamed from his mouth.

The carriage hurtled through London, reaching St Christopher's Hospital mercifully quickly. Attendants rushed out of the entrance as Jonathan hauled Alain out of the carriage, his father still thrashing around. The attendants exchanged a meaningful look with one another, then strapped Alain down to a trolley and quickly wheeled him along the corridors.

They went out through the back doors of the hospital and crossed a small square, making for a forbidding wing distanced from the rest of the hospital. Jonathan had spent countless grim days inside this building, waiting for his dad to wake up. Though he had never heard anyone call it the Darkside Ward, he was convinced that the lost, bewildered souls who roamed its hallways had all spent time in the rotten borough. This was where everything had started for Jonathan: in some ways, this wing was where he had first crossed over to Darkside.

They crashed into the reception area, where the nurse sized up the situation with one efficient glance.

"Alain Starling, isn't it?" she said. "Take him up to Room Three."

Jonathan was grateful she had recognized them. This was the only place in Lightside where people seemed to remember him. They headed upstairs, through the open wards where patients cowered and whimpered beneath their sheets, and into a private room. Once the attendants had manoeuvred Alain into bed and left the room, Jonathan's dad calmed down, his arms dropping by his sides and his fists unclenching. It wasn't long before he slumped into unconsciousness.

"Phew," said Jonathan. "It's only a mild attack."

Theresa looked shocked. "Mild?"

"This one's nothing. He should be all right in a couple of days. The bad ones lasted for months. He nearly died."

"Oh, my boy," Theresa said, her eyes filling with tears. "It must have been so hard for you."

"I got used to it. Did the crossing hurt you too?"

Theresa shook her head. "Not this time. I used to have the same pain here that Alain has in Darkside. But I've spent twelve years in a very dark place, a place that changes you. After the Bedlam, both Darkside and Lightside feel like heaven to me."

"Mum," Jonathan began hesitantly. "When we were looking for you in the Bedlam, we heard these voices in our heads. Saying horrible things. You heard that kind of thing for years. How come you didn't go mad like all the other prisoners?"

"I had something that the others didn't have."

"What?"

She squeezed him, smiling. "You. Your father. The hope that one day I'd see you again. The loudest, nastiest voices in the world couldn't have taken that away from me."

Unwilling to leave each other, Theresa and Jonathan stayed the night and the next day in Alain's room as he slept, talking quietly and munching on stale canteen sandwiches. Jonathan's mum asked him question after question, as though she was trying to learn everything about the last twelve years in a matter of hours. It was the happiest time of Jonathan's life.

Night was returning when a wave of tiredness suddenly overcame Jonathan. He failed to stifle a face-cracking yawn.

"You look dead on your feet," Theresa said, giving him a critical look. "When was the last time you had a proper night's sleep?"

"I can't remember," he replied truthfully.

"Right. Time for bed, then."

"I want to stay here!" Jonathan protested.

"You've already spent one night in that chair. You need proper rest."

"I suppose I could go back to Mrs Elwood's," Jonathan said reluctantly.

"Who?"

"Lily Elwood. You know, your friend from Darkside. She's been living near us for years."

Theresa looked confused. "I don't remember . . . so much I have forgotten. Too many years in *that* place."

"It's all right," Jonathan said comfortingly. "It'll all come back." A thought occurred to him. "Listen, why don't you stay here with Dad?"

She glanced down at her husband's now-peaceful face. "It would be nice – I'd like to be here when he wakes up. But I don't want to leave you either."

"Stay with him," Jonathan said again. "I'll be fine for one night!"

"Can you get home all right?"

Jonathan laughed. "It's Lightside, Mum. No Rippers. No vampires. No Bow Street Runners. I think I'll be OK."

As the bus followed the familiar route home, Jonathan realized that his mum was right: he was shattered. He spent most of the journey drifting in and out of consciousness, until he wasn't sure what was a dream and what was reality:

wraiths stalked down Oxford Street, their spectral fingers reaching out towards horrified late-night shoppers; carrion birds swooped down on joggers outside Regent's Park; a creature wrapped in tatty bandages wrestled with three policemen on Kilburn High Road. In a daze, Jonathan nearly missed his stop, only just slipping through the doors as they swung shut.

Back on his street, he glanced cautiously over towards his house, but there was no sign of anything untoward. If Department D were staking it out, they were well hidden. Still reluctant to take any chances, Jonathan hurried up the driveway towards Mrs Elwood's house. There were no signs of life inside, no shafts of light peeking out from behind the drawn curtains. Jonathan frowned – Mrs Elwood wasn't usually out this time of night. He tried the handle on the front door. It yawned open into a pitch-black hallway.

"Hello?" he called out. "Mrs Elwood?"

He flicked a light switch, but the hallway remained dark. The power was out. Jonathan shivered, suddenly uneasy. The house was freezing cold, radiators icy to the touch. He crept into the kitchen, his breath forming clouds in the air. A clock ticked loudly in the silence. Rummaging through the drawers beneath the sideboard, Jonathan pulled out a handful of stubby red candles.

There was a heavy thud on the window. Jonathan spun round, ready to run, only to see a tree branch banging against the glass in the wind. This was ridiculous, he told himself sternly. After all he had been through in Darkside, all the terrifying places he had been to, he was getting spooked in Mrs Elwood's kitchen. He tried to imagine what Carnegie would say if the wereman could see Jonathan now. Nothing complimentary, he thought ruefully.

He was lighting the first candle when a shape detached itself from the darkness behind the kitchen door and fell upon him. A fist swung through the gloom, connecting with the side of Jonathan's head. He fell backwards, crashing into the sideboard and spilling the candles across the linoleum. His attacker wrapped his hands around his throat, suffocating Jonathan in a stench of stale alcohol and body odour. A rough, unshaven face loomed in front of him.

"Where's the Stone?" the man hissed.

Pinned against the sideboard by his assailant's bulk, Jonathan was struggling to breathe. "What . . . stone?" he gasped.

"The Crimson Stone," the man said dully. "I followed it here. I can feel it. It's all around us. Give it back to me."

The pressure on Jonathan's windpipe was unrelenting. Bright starbursts cascaded before his eyes. As he tumbled towards unconsciousness, it sounded as though the man was talking to him from the top of a large well, rather than inches from his nose. Dark waves closed in over Jonathan's head.

"Leave him alone," a voice called out sharply.

The man whirled round. With the vice-like fingers removed from his neck, Jonathan collapsed to the floor, tears of pain running down his face. Woozily, he looked up and saw a small silhouette standing before him. It was Mrs Elwood.

"Magpie, isn't it?" she said calmly.

"How do you know me?" the man spat back.

"You don't remember me?" Mrs Elwood said quietly. "After all the years we spent together in the Wayward Orphanage as children? You picked on me for sport – made my life a misery. You and your friend Jacobs."

"Jacobs was no friend of mine," Magpie snarled. "He sold the Stone!"

"I know," Mrs Elwood said. "He sold it to me."

As his head swam, Jonathan wondered if he was hallucinating. It couldn't be Mrs Elwood talking. The Starlings' closest family friend, the little woman who had been a second mother to Jonathan throughout the years Theresa had been missing. And now she had the Crimson Stone, Darkside's most powerful talisman?

Magpie's eyes glinted in the darkness. "You've got the Stone? Where is it? Give it to me."

"As you wish," she replied. "Horace?"

The kitchen walls trembled, and Jonathan watched almost dreamily as the bricks in the far wall peeled themselves back into an archway. A deep red light emanated from the room beyond, casting a fiery outline around Horace Carmichael. In his hands, the hunchback was carrying a square piece of masonry, slightly larger than a brick, with a glowing dark-red stain.

Magpie blinked with surprise. "I know you, hunchback.

You were at the Wayward Orphanage too. You and your freaky friend here."

Carmichael nodded. "It's fitting, don't you think? After all Lily and I suffered at your hands, the taunts and the beatings we endured, that it happens to be you two who are responsible for placing this treasure in our hands – and for giving us the instrument with which we can take our revenge."

"Stop talking!" Magpie howled. "Give me the Stone!"

"With pleasure."

Horace Carmichael lifted up the Stone and whispered something under his breath. A spear of stone shot out from the wall, skewering Magpie through his back and chest. The man grunted, his body stiffening. Blood trickled from his mouth, and he slumped over the spear.

Nothing moved for a time. Then the moon drifted out from behind a cloud, drawing a bright tide of light across the kitchen. The first thing it revealed was Magpie impaled upon the stone spear, still standing, his eyes wide with shock. Jonathan's stomach churned at the sight of the puddle of blood collecting beneath the body. Then the moonlight touched on Horace Carmichael, and the look of deep satisfaction in his eyes.

"Mrs Elwood?" Jonathan called out finally, swallowing awkwardly.

"Yes?"

"What's going on?"

The dwarf came and knelt down by his side. Her hands

were trembling, and tears glistened in her eyes. She held his hand.

"I am so sorry," she whispered. "Believe me, I am."

"Sorry? You saved my life! What do you mean?"

"She means," an imperious voice replied from the doorway, "that when I've finished with you, you'll have wished she had let you die."

Everyone in the room looked up, startled, only to see the broad figure of Aurelius Holborn standing in the doorway.

21

Raquella drummed her fingers on the table, half wanting to scream with frustration. She had spent the entire day cooped up in Vendetta's townhouse, restlessly pacing the corridors whilst Sam slept and Harry flicked idly through the vampire's books. The young journalist had been unusually quiet. Raquella had been expecting him to bring up their kiss, if only to tease her about it, but he had said nothing. She found herself wishing for Carnegie and Marianne's return – even Vendetta would have provided a welcome distraction.

Clicking her tongue with irritation, Raquella went upstairs to check on Sam. The boy hadn't stirred since his fit the previous night; no more cries echoed around the townhouse. Raquella hoped the rest was doing him good. Quietly pushing open the door, she slipped inside the bedroom. And gasped.

Sam's bed was empty and the window was wide open, curtains billowing in the draught.

"Harry!" cried Raquella.

He was at her side in a second, swearing at the sight of the empty bed. "I should have seen this coming," he said grimly.

"Sam can't go outside now!" Raquella protested. "The curfew's on – if the Runners get their hands on him, there's no telling what they'll do to him! What *is* he thinking?"

"He's not thinking, Raquella," Harry replied. "His mind has been poisoned."

"Ripper knows how long he's been gone. He could be anywhere by now."

Harry poked his head out through the open window. "It might be easier to find him than you think. Look."

Crossing the room to join him, Raquella saw that a recent snowfall had laid a perfect white carpet over the deserted streets. Where the street lamps cast an orange glow on to the ground, a single trail of footprints was visible, leading from the drainpipe beneath the window deeper into Darkside.

"Do you think we can track him?"

"No one else is going to be stupid enough to be out on the streets," replied Harry. "Finding Sam would be the least of our problems."

Raquella hurried downstairs to the coat stand and donned a furred coat, hat and gloves. Harry watched her thoughtfully.

"What is it?"

He hesitated. "Look, I know you're worried about this lad, but are you sure it's wise going after him? More than likely he's come to grief already, and we're not going to help anyone by getting caught too."

A tart response came to Raquella's lips, only to die away at the look of concern on Harry's face. Instead, she said softly: "Sam's all alone, Harry. And he's not well. I can't just leave him out there."

Harry sighed. "Let me get my coat. I hear Blackchapel cells are pretty nippy this time of year."

They stole out through the front door and into the snow, ducking from doorway to doorway, breathing easier in the shelter of shadows. Sam had left a clear trail for them to follow, his footprints weaving back and forth across the road like a drunken ant. Darkside was deathly quiet: the clank of industrial machinery had been silenced; the backstreet screams of unfortunate victims no longer peppered the air. Shopfronts were shuttered; in homes, curtains covered windows like shrouds. The atmosphere was as taut as a garotte.

After half an hour of mouse-like scurrying, they found themselves in the noxious tanning district in east Darkside. Sam's footsteps were getting further apart, suggesting that he had broken into a shambling run.

Raquella suddenly tugged Harry's sleeve and pointed up into the air. "There! I see him!"

Harry looked up. Above the row of tanning factories ran a large brick viaduct, borne by a series of serpentine arches that planted themselves amongst the warren of buildings like giants' feet. On the side of the viaduct, a small figure could be seen climbing determinedly up a ladder towards the top of the bridge.

Cupping his hands together, Harry yelled "Sam!" at the top of his voice. Though the echo of the cry lingered dangerously in the street, the boy didn't stop climbing.

Raquella shot Harry a sideways glance. "Was that a wise idea?"

"Probably not," he replied defensively. "I guess we'll just have to go up after him."

As curtains began to twitch in nearby houses, they hurriedly cut through a side alley to the base of the viaduct, and the access ladder that stretched up towards the summit. Harry craned his neck as he searched out Sam, a dubious expression on his face.

"It's a long way up," he said. "You'd better go first."

"Harry Pierce," Raquella hissed, "there is no way you are climbing beneath me. I am wearing a dress, remember?"

"But then if you fall, I can catch you."

"Well, if you fall, I'll catch you," Raquella retorted. "Deal?"

Harry looked as though he was about to argue, and then thought better of it. Raquella followed him up the ladder, but it didn't take long for her to regret her decision. The metal rungs were perilously slippery to the touch, and as they climbed, the wind tugged mischievously at her clothes. Above her, Harry moved lithely and effortlessly up the ladder, aided by his Ripper-given gift of agility.

Raquella was silently cursing his nimbleness when, in

stretching for the next rung, her foot slipped beneath her. She screamed, dangling in mid-air, only the desperate grip of her left hand preventing her from plummeting down to the streets below. Then a strong hand reached down and grabbed her, hauling her back on to the ladder.

"Are you OK?" asked Harry.

Raquella clung to the rungs, breathing heavily. "Yes," she said eventually. "Thank you. Let's get this over with, shall we?"

For the rest of the climb, she concentrated solely on her ascent: first one hand, then one foot, then the other hand, then the other foot. Finally there were no more rungs to reach for, and she was able to pull herself up on to solid ground.

As she caught her breath, Raquella took in her surroundings. The viaduct cut right through the heart of Darkside, heading towards a dark tunnel carved into a hillside to the west. Beyond the edge of the bridge, slanting roofs formed a haphazard mosaic, dotted with gaping black holes like missing teeth where disrepair or bad weather had torn away the tiles. With hours to go until sunrise and the lifting of the curfew, the twisting alleyways were empty. Even so, from this height there was a certain grimy grandeur to the borough.

A diminutive figure was trudging along the bridge in the distance – Sam. His progress was looking increasingly laborious, and it wasn't long before they caught up with him.

"Sam!" Raquella called out. As she clutched his arm, she felt goosebumps beneath his thin shirt. He stopped reluctantly, barely seeming to recognize her. "What on Darkside are you doing up here?"

"Following the Stone," Sam replied dully. "It's this way."

"You must be freezing! Why don't you come back to the townhouse with us?"

Sam shook his head. "Need the Stone. Going to get it."

"Now, come on, Sam—"

"Hold on, Raquella," Harry said suddenly. "Maybe he's right. Maybe we shouldn't go back."

The maid shot him a questioning glance.

"Look, we don't know what's happened to Carnegie and Marianne," Harry continued, counting off his fingers. "Jonathan's gone. Ripper only knows where Vendetta is. For all we know, it could just be the three of us left. And what can we do to stop Lucien then? But if Sam can track down the Crimson Stone, that might even up the odds a bit, don't you think?"

"But we've no idea what the Stone can do, Harry! Or who's got it now!"

"Think about it, Raquella. What have we got to lose?"

The maid tapped her foot thoughtfully, then shook her head in resignation. "I don't know why I let you talk me into these sorts of things."

With a smile, Harry draped his coat over Sam's shoulders. "Lead the way, then, lad," he said kindly.

Sam turned away and carried on along the viaduct, the

oversized coat dragging through the snow. As they followed behind him, Raquella slipped her cold hand into Harry's. If it hadn't been for the threat of danger hanging over them, and the icy wind lashing their skin, the moonlit walk would have been almost picturesque.

At one point the snow thinned, and Raquella stubbed her toe on something solid. Biting back an oath, she stooped over and brushed away the snow.

"There are train tracks down here!" she said, surprised.

"Really?" replied Harry. He frowned. "That's funny – I've never seen a train run up here. Maybe it used to be part of the Dark Line. You wouldn't believe some of the reasons why bits of *that* line closed. I worked on a story once for the *Informer* where this zombie conductor— Hey, what is it?"

Raquella had stopped and looked back, the wind blowing strands of hair across her face.

"Can you hear anything?" she asked.

"Probably just the wind," Harry said. "It's pretty wild up here."

They walked a few paces further before Raquella stopped again. "No, I can definitely hear something. Listen."

Straining his ears above the keening wind, Harry could just about make out a faint roaring sound. He peered into the darkness.

"Can't see anything," he reported.

"There's definitely something coming this way," Raquella said nervously. "Look at the tracks."

The rusty rails had begun to quiver beneath their feet.

The roaring was getting louder. Harry's heart quickened. Looking back now, he could see a shape moving quickly along the viaduct.

"I thought you said you'd never seen a train up here!" Raquella shouted.

"That's not a train," Harry replied grimly.

The surface of the viaduct was churning up behind them, forming a peak in the centre of the bridge that looked like a shark's fin. It was hurtling towards them at great speed.

"It's a Runner!" yelled Harry. "Come on!"

They broke into a headlong sprint, adrenaline coursing through their veins. Dimly aware of the danger, Sam had broken into a faltering run, his coat falling from his shoulders as he stumbled onwards. They looked down at the ground as they ran, trying to avoid tripping over the treacherous railway sleepers.

The western hillside rose up before them, only a hundred metres away now. Behind them, the Runner ploughed remorselessly through the ground, sending rivets popping into the air like champagne corks.

"It's gaining on us!" Raquella cried.

"Try and get to the tunnel!" Harry shouted back. "Maybe we can lose it there."

The ground rippled beneath their feet as the Runner closed in for the kill. Risking a glance over his shoulder, Harry made out a face amidst the tidal wave of bricks, its mouth yawning open.

When they arrived at the mouth of the tunnel, they were greeted by a cavernous archway that rose high above their heads. As the Runner exploded out of the ground, two giant arms reaching out for them, they dived headlong into the darkness.

22

After tumbling into the dirt, Harry rolled over and sprang quickly back to his feet. He'd expected the Bow Street Runner to be bearing down upon him, but to his surprise he saw that it had halted at the mouth of the tunnel, as though blocked by some invisible wall. In a rage, the Runner punched the ground so hard that its fist crashed through the ground, showering pebbles and rocks everywhere. Then it dived beneath the surface with an angry roar, the viaduct trembling as the Runner disappeared from sight.

As the adrenaline drained from his system, Harry was suddenly aware of a throbbing pain in his head and a nauseous feeling in the pit of his stomach. Scanning the dingy tunnel for Raquella and Sam, he spotted the maid lying face down by the side of the tracks.

"Raquella!"

He raced over and knelt down beside her. The maid was dazed, a bruise on her forehead where she had banged her head. She stirred as Harry cradled her.

"Are you OK?" he asked.

"Just about," she replied faintly. "What happened to the Runner?"

"I don't know," Harry replied. "It couldn't follow us down the tunnel."

"We've crossed over to Lightside," said Sam. The little boy was sitting cross-legged on the train tracks, a distant expression on his face. "The Runners are a part of Darkside itself – they can't exist beyond its borders."

"How do you know?" Raquella asked.

"They're linked to the Stone. They miss it too, just like me." Sam got to his feet. "We should go. It's not that far away now."

The little boy walked away down the passage without another word. Gently helping Raquella to her feet, Harry set off after him.

The tracks sloped sharply downwards as the tunnel burrowed deeper and deeper into the hillside. This far from the surface, there was a wild timelessness to their surroundings that made the teenagers feel small and insignificant. Jagged stalactites hung down from the ceiling, an armoury of giant rocky daggers. A cascade of water gushed out from a spring, picking out a glinting trail of minerals amidst the rocks in its path. Labyrinthine spiders' webs draped the walls like tapestries, while the cavern's recesses reverberated to the sound of scuttling animals.

Just as Harry's knees were getting sore from navigating the steep slope, the tunnel levelled out. Here the natural rock formations had been wrestled under control, moulded into a low vaulted ceiling and smooth walls. The tunnel curved, and as they rounded the bend, a low railway platform came into view on the right-hand side of the tracks. An old-fashioned street lamp was burning brightly, showing a series of archways leading off into the gloom. At the far end of the platform, a wrought-iron spiral staircase rose into the air.

They walked up the sloped edge of the platform, relieved to leave the tracks. Above each of the archways, a mixture of Darkside and Lightside place names had been daubed in black paint: Whitechapel, the Cain Club, Hampstead Heath, Bleakmoor, the Houses of Parliament.

Harry let out a low whistle. "You can travel all over London from here!"

Raquella began brushing a thick layer of cobwebs away from a large sign screwed into the wall, gradually revealing the word "Jackwalk" in a series of florid letters etched into the metal.

"'Jackwalk'?" she said, puzzled. "Where on earth are we?"

"I don't know," Harry called back. "It looks like some kind of abandoned Underground station. Jonathan says there's loads of them in Lightside."

Sam tapped his foot impatiently as his companions explored their surroundings. Harry gave the boy a shrewd look. "You know what this place is, don't you?"

"It's Jackwalk," shrugged Sam, as though it was obvious. "The first Ripper's private route into Lightside."

"How do you know?"

For the first time since his rescue from the Bedlam, Sam smiled. "Jack used the Crimson Stone to build it, transforming solid rock into caverns and tunnels. I can still feel the walls trembling. Using this network, Jack could travel to all parts of London and never be seen. It came in handy when he had secret midnight meetings with Lightside criminals or politicians. Or when he wanted to kill."

The thought of following in a murderer's footsteps as he hunted for victims made Raquella shiver. "I'm surprised word never got out about this place."

Sam shook his head. "Jack guarded his secrets jealously. He didn't even tell his sons about it. The Runners knew, because they were linked to the Stone, but they lay dormant most of the time, and they can't leave Darkside anyway."

"So we're the first people to see this place since Jack himself?" asked Harry.

"I wouldn't be so sure about that," Raquella replied, pointedly glancing up at the street lamp. "Unless this has been burning for a century, someone's been down here recently."

"It doesn't matter," Sam said blankly. "The Stone is what's important. It's very near now. I can feel it." He pointed up the winding spiral staircase. "We need to go this way."

They began to climb up the staircase, the dull ring of their footfalls on the iron steps echoing around Jackwalk. Remembering her struggles on the viaduct ladder, Raquella held firmly on to the railing as they spiralled higher and higher into the air. Sam trudged on in the lead, seemingly unaware of anything save the proximity of the Crimson Stone.

The staircase came to an abrupt end at a plain door that swung open when Harry pushed on it. To his amazement, he found himself standing on a narrow walkway overlooking a long, lavish study. Down below them, the marbled floor was dotted with glass display cases, while the ornately carved walls were lined with books and curios. After they had all filed out on to the walkway, Raquella closed the door behind them – it fitted into a wooden façade so seamlessly that it was impossible to see the join, let alone guess what lay on the other side.

Before they could take another step, the sound of voices drifted up from the ground floor. Raquella cast a quizzical glance at Harry, who put his finger to his lips in reply. He peered over the guard rail, his eyes widening with surprise.

A host of figures were walking through the gloomy gallery. There, in the middle of them, was Jonathan Starling.

They had travelled through London in Mrs Elwood's car: the dwarf bolstered by a cushion on her seat, her specially adapted pedals reaching up towards her feet. Jonathan was wedged in the back seat between Horace Carmichael and Holborn, his hands bound tightly behind his back. The atmosphere was tense, the Abettor's unexpected appearance at Mrs Elwood's house apparently surprising Carmichael as much as Jonathan. For his part, Holborn was visibly annoyed by the fact that the Crimson Stone remained in the detective's lap.

"I am the Abettor," he had argued. "It should fall to me to pass the Crimson Stone to Lucien. You have no right to keep hold of it."

"Your bluster won't work on me," Carmichael replied calmly. "I work for Lucien, not you: I'll pass it to him. If you want to try and take the Stone from me, go ahead."

Holborn had flashed the hunchback a dark look, but let the matter drop.

Still reeling from Mrs Elwood's betrayal, Jonathan barely felt the ropes biting into his wrists. Throughout Jonathan's childhood the tiny woman had been the one constant in his life, the only reliable source of care and attention. And now she was sending him to his doom. Jonathan's mum and dad were in the hospital, and Carnegie, Marianne and the others were back in Darkside – there was no one left to rescue him.

The car's engine purred like a cat as the vehicle prowled the leafy squares of Bloomsbury in central London. Mrs Elwood turned left on to a narrow street, bringing the car to a halt outside a long railing. Through the gaps in the bars, and past the wide expanse of the courtyard beyond, Jonathan saw a set of stone steps sweeping up towards a giant neoclassical building fronted by a stone colonnade. Bright floodlights lit up the pillars in front of the main entrance.

"The British Museum?" Jonathan said, surprise in his voice. "What are we doing here?"

"Keeping our mouths shut," Carmichael said threateningly. The hunchback climbed awkwardly out of the car door, weighed down by the Crimson Stone. "If you start shouting for help, you're going to end up like Magpie – understand?"

Jonathan nodded. There wasn't any other choice. He allowed Holborn to haul him out of the car, then followed the Abettor through the wide-open gates and across the courtyard. Mrs Elwood trotted along at the back of the group, her short legs struggling to keep pace.

Two bulky figures were standing guard by the doorway to the museum. As he walked up the steps, Jonathan recognized the two fire salamanders from the hospital.

Holborn gave Carmichael a sideways glance. "It would seem we are expected."

"I called ahead to arrange everything," the detective replied. "Given our precious cargo, I thought it best that we weren't bothered by security guards."

He nodded briskly at the salamanders, who stared unblinkingly back at him, their black scales gleaming in the floodlights. They took up a position on either side of Jonathan, then followed the hunchback through the main door and inside the museum.

"I still don't get why we're here," Jonathan said, bemused.

"There is a crossing point within these walls," Holborn replied regally. "I used it earlier today with that wretched tramp, Magpie. It holds the distinct advantage of taking us directly back to Blackchapel. There is no time to waste – I guarantee that Lucien is itching to see you. Not only do you owe him for ruining his Night Hunt, but both he – and I – are very interested in the current whereabouts of Marianne."

"I'm not telling you anything," retorted Jonathan.

"We'll see, Starling," Holborn said ominously.

As they crossed a vast indoor courtyard, priceless exhibits shrouded in darkness, Mrs Elwood scurried over to Carmichael, her eyes shining. "How do you feel holding the Stone?" she whispered. "Amazing, isn't it?"

"It feels strange," Carmichael replied uncertainly. "I feel . . . connected to everything . . . the ground and the walls, like they're extensions of my arms and legs. I think I could bring down the museum around us if I wanted."

"Stop that!" snapped Holborn. "The Stone is too powerful to be trifled with. It can raze buildings at a thought."

"And you're going to hand it over to Lucien," Jonathan said to Carmichael, a look of disgust on his face. "Imagine what he'll do with it."

The hunchback shrugged in the gloom. "That isn't really my concern. My job is to keep the equilibrium between Darkside and Lightside. Lucien's unpopularity is threatening everything – but if he has the Stone, no one can stop him. If he is grateful enough to reward me, then all the better."

"Naturally," Holborn replied smoothly. Even in the darkness, Jonathan had noticed that the Abettor couldn't help hungrily glancing at the Stone.

"Are you OK, Jonathan?"

It was Mrs Elwood speaking, her face creased with concern.

"What do you care?" Jonathan said. "Leave me alone."

She looked down at her feet. "I don't expect you to understand," she said quietly. "You don't know what it was like for Horace and me growing up. A hunchback and a dwarf: even in Darkside, it made us easy targets. But the more the other children laughed at us, the closer we became. He looked after me like I was his sister. We lost track of one another when we were teenagers, and I didn't even know Horace was on Lightside until I saw him search your house. But from that moment, my path was clear. I had to help Horace, no matter what the cost."

"I still don't understand," said Jonathan. "When you first met us, you told us that you were friends with my mum. But that wasn't true, was it? Why did you lie? Why us?"

Mrs Elwood sighed. "When your father was working in the watch shop in Darkside, I lived in the house opposite. I used to watch him through the window as he worked. Back then, Alain seemed so happy and content: I envied him so. When I heard about Theresa's disappearance, I wondered if there was now room in his life for me. I travelled to Lightside and pretended to be an old friend of your mother's. He was so desperate for any kind of link to her, he didn't take much convincing."

"You lied," Jonathan said fiercely. "All those years, and it was all lies."

An odd look crossed the dwarf's face. "At the beginning,

yes. But as the time passed, I came to believe my story as though it was the truth. Eventually I loved you like you were my own child. I never thought for a second that Theresa might still be alive. I tried to persuade Alain to move on, to try not to return to Darkside, but he never gave up. And then you discovered a way over."

"You would have been advised to stay where you were," Holborn intoned. "You tried to meddle with affairs that didn't concern you. And now you're going to pay the price." Leaning closer, he said in a low whisper: "Have you seen the Black Phoenix when it flies in for the kill? It is a sight of truly terrifying beauty. You should be honoured, child."

Jonathan shuddered. He still had nightmares about facing the Black Phoenix, and the feeling of terror as its cloud of fear smothered him.

"Stop tormenting the lad," Carmichael said sharply. "His fate is dark enough without your gloating."

An angry look flashed across Holborn's face, but he said nothing. Having left the indoor courtyard, the group was now threading its way through a narrow gallery. Jonathan was wondering whether he should try to make a run for it when he heard a familiar voice cry out his name.

"Look out!" shouted Raquella.

Glancing up, he saw a silhouette swooping through the air, and then Harry Pierce came crashing down upon them.

23

Harry yelled a war cry as he landed upon the group, the force of his impact scattering them like skittles. As a surprised Holborn collided into him, Jonathan fell to the floor, only just managing to scramble out of the way as one of the fire salamanders tumbled over. Horace Carmichael went staggering to one side, the weight of the Crimson Stone propelling him into one of the glass display cases with a deafening crash. The hunchback slumped down into a bleeding heap, the Stone spilling from his grasp. Mrs Elwood screamed.

With his hands still bound behind his back, it was difficult for Jonathan to get back on to his feet. The nearest salamander stretched out to grab his leg; he wriggled across the floor and out of reach. There was a tug on his shoulder, and then Harry hauled him to his feet.

"Let's get out of here!" Harry shouted.

Jonathan stumbled away through the gallery, shouts of confusion ringing in his ears.

"After them!" bellowed Holborn.

Risking a glance over his shoulder, Jonathan saw that the fire salamanders had dropped down on to all fours and were scuttling after them, their heads low to the ground, their tongues hungrily tasting the air.

Jonathan and Harry zigzagged frantically through the museum, hurtling up staircases and along hallways, all the while pursued by the ominous patter of reptilian feet. Running past one gloomy exhibit after another, Jonathan felt surrounded by death: Egyptian mummies lay entombed in ornate sarcophagi, preserved for eternity; tribal death masks with empty eyeholes leered down from the walls; the remains of ancient corpses curled up inside glass boxes, shrivelled brown tangles of bone.

As they raced along a narrow corridor hemmed in by backlit display cases, Harry skidded to a halt.

"Wait!"

He smashed the glass of the nearest case with his elbow, reached inside and pulled free an antique dagger. As Harry hacked through the ropes around his wrists, Jonathan saw that his friend's shirtsleeve was torn, revealing a patch of blotchy, red-raw skin.

"What happened to your arm?"

"It's nothing," said Harry. "I touched one of those salamanders when I jumped on top of you. I forgot their skin was poisonous. Keep them at arm's length if you can."

"I'll do my best." Jonathan grinned. "That was some leap back there."

Harry looked rueful. "Thanks. I'm not sure it was my cleverest idea, but it was the best I could come up with at the time." He glanced along the empty corridor, alert for any sign of the enemy. "Now you're free, we need to get back to the gallery. It looks like we've lost the salamanders, and we've left Raquella and Sam behind in the same room as Holborn and Carmichael."

"They're not safe there."

"You're telling me." Harry chewed on his lip thoughtfully. "You know, we could really do with some more weapons."

He turned and began to inspect the display cases. As Jonathan rubbed his chafing wrists, there was a gleam of orange in the doorway, and a scaly head nosed its way around the corner. Jonathan slowly tapped his friend on the shoulder.

"Harry? I think the salamanders have found us again."

At that moment, a woman's blood-curling scream echoed throughout the museum.

Raquella's heart was in her mouth as she watched Jonathan and Harry flee from the gallery, the salamanders crawling menacingly after them. As the sounds of commotion disappeared down the hallways, the room went quiet again. Horace Carmichael was sprawled on the ground, blood trickling from a head wound. Mrs Elwood crouched by his side, holding his hand and whispering tenderly into his ear.

There was a movement in the darkness as Holborn slowly rose to his feet and walked over to where the Crimson

Stone lay. The Abettor picked up the precious artefact, running his fingers over it with a sharp intake of breath. By Raquella's side, Sam moaned unhappily – she grabbed hold of his wrist, preventing him from going down after the Stone.

"Ripper be praised!" murmured Holborn. "Such power!"

Carmichael rolled over with a groan. "Forget the boys," he said to the Abettor weakly. "Get out of here now – take the Stone to Lucien as fast as you can."

"Oh, you can count on that," Holborn breathed. "Lucien will discover the might of the Crimson Stone all too soon."

"What do you mean by that?" asked Mrs Elwood.

Holborn smiled thinly. "Let's just say that this Ripper's reign will be as long as his death will be lamented."

"What?" Carmichael looked up sharply, wincing with pain. "You're going to set yourself against Lucien?"

"Count on it."

"But think of all we fought for! We stopped Vendetta raising Lucien's brother from the dead! We helped Lucien defeat Marianne. Don't throw it away now!"

"I don't know what petty reasons governed your choice of sides," Holborn said, with a sneer. "I was always building towards this moment. Now, with the Stone under my control, Darkside will be mine."

"Your ambition will be the death of you, Abettor," said Carmichael. "Mark my words."

"Perhaps. You needn't worry about it, though. It is no concern of yours any longer."

As the Abettor stood over Carmichael and Mrs Elwood, it seemed to the watching Raquella that he was somehow growing in size and stature, his broad shoulders casting a lengthening shadow across the gallery floor. Mrs Elwood whimpered as Holborn lifted the Stone high into the air.

"Do what you must with me," Carmichael said through clenched teeth. "But leave Lily alone. This is nothing to do with her."

"What?" Holborn exclaimed mockingly. "And split the two of you up, so soon after you have found each other again? I could never be so cruel."

As the Abettor muttered something under his breath, the ground beneath Mrs Elwood and Horace Carmichael suddenly caved in, the marbled surface dissolving into a swirling whirlpool. It was as though someone had pulled a plug out from beneath the museum. Raquella watched in horror as Carmichael was sucked underground with a loud gurgling noise; with a piercing scream, Mrs Elwood followed him beneath the earth, her hands clawing vainly for something to cling on to. When they had both vanished from view, the floor closed over their heads, re-forming into a smooth surface that left no trace of either the hunchback or the dwarf.

Holborn nodded with murderous satisfaction. Smoothing down his robe, he strode out of the gallery and made his way up to the first-floor walkway. Raquella clamped her hand over Sam's mouth and hastily drew back into a shadowy niche. She held her breath as the Abettor marched past, summoning all her strength to restrain Sam as he reached out longingly towards the Stone. The secret entrance to Jackwalk clicked open, and then Holborn was gone.

The salamander crept towards Jonathan and Harry, its beady eyes glinting. They backed away down the corridor and into a large exhibition room, their eyes fixed unwaveringly on the creature. Display cases loomed out of the dark around them like large glass obelisks.

"What do we do now?" Jonathan said, out of the corner of his mouth.

"Stall it," Harry whispered back. "I'll be back in a second."

"What?"

Harry scampered away before he could call him back. Swearing under his breath, Jonathan turned back to face the salamander. How was he supposed to stall it – he couldn't even touch it!

The creature had stopped advancing and was eyeing him intently. Jonathan frowned. What was it waiting for?

There was a hiss at his shoulder.

Jonathan ducked instinctively as the second salamander lunged at him from the side, jaws snapping. The creature swung a fist through the space where his head had been seconds before, shattering the glass in the display case behind him.

Rolling to one side before the salamander could pounce on him, Jonathan scurried away between the exhibits on his hands and knees, his heart pounding furiously. In the watchful silence, he could hear the two creatures exhaling, and the soft tread of their feet on the wooden floorboards.

Jonathan crawled around the corner of a display case – and found himself face to face with the mottled black and orange features of a salamander. It grinned devilishly.

"Harry!" he shouted. "Help!"

"I'm coming!" came the reply.

Harry Pierce came tearing along the main aisle of the exhibition room, a sturdy stick in his hands. Digging the stick into the ground, he vaulted over the display case by Jonathan, landing neatly on two feet with gymnastic precision. Before the salamander could react, Harry swung the stick high above his head and delivered a crushing blow to the creature's skull. It crumpled lifelessly to the floor.

Harry wiped the end of the stick matter-of-factly on the ground. "Told you we needed a weapon. I found this on the wall. Now, let's see where the other one's hiding."

He slipped away, cutting a stealthy path through the exhibits like a big-game hunter on safari. Jonathan stayed close behind him, his mind turning every unusual shadow into a monster.

The second salamander leapt between them without warning. Harry tumbled backwards in surprise, dropping his stick. The creature ignored him, lunging at Jonathan as he turned on his heel and ran. Jonathan weaved a frantic path through the display cases, aware that the salamander was closing in on him.

Dodging away from a poisonous swipe, he ducked left down a narrow aisle, only to crash into a metal guard rail. Beyond it lay a steep drop to the courtyard in the centre of the museum. Jonathan had run straight into a dead end.

The salamander slowed as it followed him around the corner, hissing in triumph. Seeing the creature's muscles tense, Jonathan waited until the salamander launched itself towards him, then dived to one side. He felt a singe of pain as the creature brushed his side; then the fire salamander tumbled over the rail and hurtled down to the floor below, hitting the ground with a loud squelch.

Jonathan wearily pulled himself up to the rail and looked down to see the salamander spreadeagled across the museum floor, orange slime oozing from its carcass. Harry appeared at his side, and patted him on the back. "Nice move," he said approvingly. "Now let's go get the others."

They raced back to the gallery to find Raquella struggling to keep Sam away from the secret door leading back to Jackwalk.

"Are you all right?" Harry asked urgently. "We heard a scream."

The maid looked at Jonathan, her eyes serious. "It was Mrs Elwood. She and Carmichael are dead."

Jonathan felt a knife twist in his soul. Even after everything that had happened, he had loved Mrs Elwood for too many years not to feel a sharp pain at her death.

"What happened?" he asked quietly.

"Holborn double-crossed them," Raquella replied. "He

took the Stone and killed them, then went back to Darkside. He's going to take on Lucien himself."

A spark of anger ignited within Jonathan. "Right. Come on then."

"Where are we going?"

"After Holborn," replied Jonathan. "This isn't over yet."

Sam eagerly raced back up towards the walkway, leading them through the secret door and back into the vast cavern beyond. They hurried down the spiral staircase to the platform, where the street lamp was burning low. There was no sign of Holborn. Glancing at the passageways sloping off in different directions, Harry scratched his head.

"How do we know which way he went?"

Jonathan stopped beneath the archway marked "Blackchapel". "He's going after Lucien, isn't he? He must have gone this way."

The tunnel beyond the archway was pitch-black. The four children paused, waiting for their eyes to get accustomed to the light.

"Jonathan!" Raquella cried suddenly. "He's right here!"

Straining his eyes through the darkness, Jonathan made out the outline of the Abettor blocking the passageway in front of them.

"I heard the sound of rats upon the stairs," Holborn said. "Thought I'd better stop and deal with them. Horrible things, rats. Wouldn't want them infesting Blackchapel – especially not when I'm this close to claiming my throne."

"It's not your throne," Jonathan said fiercely. "Or

Lucien's. It's Marianne's. And we're going to make sure she gets it."

The Abettor gave out a booming laugh. "Such bold words! And how do you propose to stop me? Do you not understand the power I now have at my fingertips? Let me give you a demonstration."

With that, he pressed the Crimson Stone against the wall. The tunnel entrance shook, and chunks of masonry began to rain down from the ceiling.

"He's started a cave-in!" cried Jonathan. "Look out!"

As Harry grabbed Sam and dived back on to the platform, Jonathan pushed Raquella to safety. Before he could join them, a heavy piece of stone crashed into his left shoulder, knocking him to the floor. The last thing Jonathan saw, through the falling rubble, was the figure of Holborn hurrying away, and then the world collapsed around him in a cloud of dust.

For a few seconds the Jackwalk platform was enveloped in a shocked silence. Harry stared at the entrance to the Blackchapel tunnel, which was completely blocked by rubble, a choking cloud of dust rising into the air. Then he began scrabbling in the debris, throwing rocks to one side.

"Jonathan!" he cried out. "Are you there?"

There was a faint coughing sound, and then a muffled voice said from within the tunnel: "It's all right."

Raquella's shoulders sagged with relief. "Are you hurt?"

"I'm OK," Jonathan replied. "I don't think I've broken

anything. But there are rocks everywhere – it's going to take me a while to get free. Go on without me."

"We can't leave you on your own!" Harry protested.

"There isn't anything you can do here. I'll follow Holborn back to Blackchapel this way. You need to get back to Darkside. There's no time to waste."

Harry chewed his lip in consternation. "It's going to take us ages to get back over the viaduct," he said. "We'll never catch up with Holborn in time. We're stuck."

"No, we're not."

Raquella and Harry spun round and looked at Sam.

"I know Jackwalk too, remember?" the boy said quietly. "If we take the right path, we can catch up with Holborn."

"Which path?" Harry asked urgently.

Sam pointed to his left, at a crumbling archway beneath a sign time had long since eroded away.

"Come on," Harry said grimly. "It's time to end this."

24

Although the Great Riot of Darkside became one of the most celebrated events in the borough's history, in the years that followed, no one could agree on exactly how it had begun, which spark had started the blaze. Some claimed that it had spiralled from an argument between two urchins over a dead cat; others, rather more grandly, said that a nobleman had started the uprising with the aim of rescuing his beloved from the Blackchapel cells. The only thing people could agree on was that they had all played prominent roles. Decades later, elderly Darksiders enthralled their grandchildren with epic tales of their own involvement, regardless of whether or not they had actually been there – or even been alive at the time.

No matter how it started, by midnight the Grand was engulfed by a writhing sea of people: men and women, the old and the young, engaged in a mass brawl that ran the length of Darkside's main street. After days of pent-up frustration and nights trapped behind closed doors, there was a joyful edge to the anarchy. Punches were traded with relish, whoops of delight intermingling with shouts of agony in the violent pandemonium. From time to time the sound of shattering glass elicited a throaty roar from the crowd: looters broke into shops and returned, arms laden with goods, only to be mugged on the pavement outside. The telltale glow of fire was visible within one or two of the buildings, flames clawing at the woodwork.

At the top of the Grand, two figures stood on the side of an upturned carriage, calmly looking down upon the chaos. Carnegie and Marianne had returned from the Wayward Orphanage to find the townhouse completely empty. Unsure if they should cross over to Lightside in search of Jonathan, they had been arguing over their next move when the first sounds of disturbance reached them. Without a word, they changed out of their disguises and into their normal clothes: Carnegie smiled with satisfaction as he adjusted the towering stovepipe hat on his head, while Marianne tied her freshly dyed white hair back into a ponytail and methodically checked the array of weapons concealed within her clothing.

As they watched, there was a loud boom. Several streets away, a grimy mushroom cloud rose into the air. The wereman jumped.

"What on Darkside was that?"

Marianne peered into the night. "I think some idiot's torched Chang's Wonders of the Orient."

"Then that's the last mistake they'll ever make," Carnegie

growled. "There's enough gunpowder in the fireworks in that shop to take out half the street."

"This doesn't make any sense," Marianne said, frowning as she surveyed the carnage. "Where are the Runners?"

"There's only two options," replied Carnegie. "Either Lucien's decided out of the kindness of his heart to take the Runners off the streets . . ."

"Somewhat unlikely."

". . . or there's a greater threat to the Ripper that demands the Runners' attention."

"Greater threat than the whole of the borough rioting?" Marianne asked. "This I have to see. I think a quick trip to Blackchapel is in order."

Carnegie swept off his stovepipe hat, bowing as he gestured towards the battle-strewn street. "Shall we?"

"Charmed, I'm sure," Marianne said lightly.

They jumped down from the carriage and strode down the Grand. Carnegie cracked his knuckles and rotated his neck muscles, while Marianne drew her sword from her sheath. Heads turned at their approach – all about them, the fighting came to an abrupt halt.

"It's the Marianne imposter!" a voice cried out. "She's mine!"

"Stay away from her!" a gruff voice replied. "She's mine!"

As a ring of Darksiders tightened menacingly around them, Marianne sighed. "I'd forgotten all about that blasted reward. This promises to be quite a tiresome journey."

Carnegie gave her a wolfish grin. "I wouldn't say that," he said.

With a snarl, he hurled himself at two burly stevedores, raking their faces with his claws and forcing them backwards. At such close quarters, there was no room for finesse: as a tusked creature grabbed at Marianne, she poked him in the eye and thumped him on the head with the hilt of her sword, before swivelling round and taking a cut-throat's legs out from under him with a sweeping kick.

Carnegie and Marianne inched their way along the Grand, held up by the sheer weight of numbers. Every time an assailant was downed, two sprang forward to take their place, spurred on by their desire to claim the vast reward on Marianne's head.

"As fun as this is," Carnegie growled, punching a hoodlum in the face almost absent-mindedly, "it's going to slow us down a bit."

Marianne ducked out of the way of a clumsy haymaker, then sharply kneed her attacker in the groin. The man collapsed in a heap, his face turning a sickly green colour.

"I agree," she shouted back. "Let's take a short cut."

Reaching inside her jacket, she pulled out a small glass bottle and sprayed a fine mist over herself. Before the wereman could argue, she turned and squirted him with the perfume as well. Carnegie bayed with displeasure, rubbing his eyes.

"Oh, do stop whining," Marianne said. "No point in me being invisible if you still have to battle your way up the Grand."

The wereman gave himself a suspicious sniff. "I smell like a duchess," he muttered.

Marianne smoothly sheathed her sword – masked by her special perfume, there was no need to fight any more. A clear path opened up along the centre of the Grand as combatants unconsciously stepped aside for them. They walked through the middle of the riot as if it were nothing more than a Sunday park stroll. From time to time Carnegie would see someone gasp with surprise and raise a club or a cosh to attack them, but they would stop mid-swing, a puzzled expression on their face, then turn to attack someone else.

The further they went along the Grand, the higher the flames rose into the night sky; the thicker the clouds of smoke billowed. No building was safe: not Kinski's Theatre of the Macabre, engulfed in a crackling cremation; nor the Aurora Borealis Candle Shop, dying a pungent, beautiful death as a thousand coloured tallows caught fire; not even the Psychosis Club, where smoke swirled out of the front door and inside a lone violin played a funereal lament.

Marianne shook her head. "At this rate, the fools are going to burn Darkside down to the ground."

"They don't care any more," said Carnegie. "Better no Darkside than Lucien's Darkside."

The fighting was getting more frenzied as the fury of the mob boiled over. Still there was no sign of the Bow Street Runners. At the crossroads near the top of the Grand, Carnegie and Marianne turned right on to Pell Mell. The bounty hunter suddenly stopped and pointed.

"Look!" she cried out. "It's my nephew!"

Harry Pierce was standing at the entrance to a side alley, shielding Raquella and Sam from two leering hobgoblins with a metal pole. Striding through the crowd, Carnegie grabbed the hobgoblins by their lank hair, cracking their heads together with a sickening thud. They slumped to the ground, blood trickling from their ears. Harry looked startled, as though he had been saved by a ghost.

"What happened?" Raquella shouted, looking straight through Carnegie.

"I don't know!" Harry shouted back.

Marianne stepped forward and sprayed them with her perfume bottle. Harry blinked, then broke into a broad grin.

"Marianne!" he said. "Am I glad to see you!"

"Likewise," she replied. "What on Darkside are you doing here?"

"It's a long story," Harry replied. "We went to Lightside to try and get the Crimson Stone, but we failed. Holborn's got it now, and he's going to Blackchapel to take on Lucien. Jonathan's gone after him – we got separated by a cave-in."

"Cave-in?" Carnegie barked. "Is the boy all right?"

Harry nodded. "I think so. But we need to get to Blackchapel as quickly as possible – we can't leave him on his own there."

"Well, let's go and give him a hand then," said Carnegie. "Come on."

Pell Mell was quieter than the Grand, the vast shadow

of Blackchapel deterring the locals from joining the riot. The Ripper's palace stood unmoved at the end of the road, its soaring walls dominating the horizon. Behind them, the rioters had stopped fighting amongst themselves, rallying to cries of "Down with Lucien!" and "Three cheers for conspiracies!" A dishevelled order fell over them as they lit torches and armed themselves with makeshift weapons.

"They've lost it," Carnegie muttered. "They're going to try and storm Blackchapel."

"Then we'd better hurry up," Marianne replied. "My perfume doesn't last for ever, and I don't want to get caught in between that lot and Lucien."

They hurried up Pell Mell and out on to the broad plaza in front of the palace. Save for the nooses swinging ominously in the breeze beneath the Tyburn Tree, everything was suddenly very still. The atmosphere crackled with impending violence.

To her surprise, Raquella saw that the iron gates leading into Blackchapel were resting open.

"Look!" she called out. "The gates are open!"

"With that mob on our tail, they won't be for long," Carnegie growled. "Move!"

Even as they raced across the plaza, there was a loud creaking noise, and the gates began to swing shut. Carnegie loped ahead of the group, jamming himself into the narrowing gap. Harry followed hot on his heels, diving past the wereman and inside the palace grounds. Slowed by the exhausted Sam, Raquella was struggling to cover the distance. Carnegie roared with effort, sweat pouring down his brow as the gates squashed him.

"Can't . . . hold . . . much . . . longer. . ."

Seeing Sam struggling, Marianne grabbed the boy and hurled him inside Blackchapel. The bounty hunter ushered Raquella through, then, as Carnegie let the gates go with a howl of pain, rolled through the gap a second before they banged shut.

"That was close," Harry said, panting.

Carnegie shot him a baleful glance. "You think? You weren't the one being squashed to a pulp."

Blackchapel's courtyard was a bleak open space where no flower or plant could flourish. Snow had been cleared from the grey gravel path that led to the palace. Blackchapel itself was as awesome as it was awful: an enormous Gothic cathedral imbued with a sense of numb horror, as though every stone, every piece of gravel had been witness to an awful crime of one sort or another.

In the silence, the first sounds of the approaching mob could be heard in the distance.

"What now?" asked Harry.

Marianne gestured towards the palace. "Let's go inside and find my dear brother. I'm sure he's dying to see us."

They were halfway up the gravel path when the courtyard erupted. All around them walls shuddered and trembled as hands and feet burst from them, snatching at the air. Suddenly the walls were alive with limbs as an entire platoon of Bow Street Runners pulled themselves free and surrounded the group.

"Damnit!" Carnegie swore. "It's a trap!"

"And I think these guys can see us," said Harry.

"Could do with some more of that perfume of yours, Marianne," Carnegie said, through clenched teeth.

The bounty hunter glanced down at her glass bottle. "Ah. May be a problem there. I used the last of it on my nephew."

"Then we're dead men," the wereman replied.

Marianne, Harry and Carnegie spread out into a triangle, protecting Raquella and Sam. The bounty hunter drew her sword and pulled a crossbow from its strapping on her back. The Runners didn't respond, scattering the snow with soot as they breathed quietly.

"Why aren't they attacking?" Harry said, out of the corner of his mouth.

He didn't have to wait long for an answer. With a crash, the doors to Blackchapel were flung open and a slight figure hobbled out, dressed in a deep-red cloak lined with fur.

Lucien Ripper smiled, his mouth curled with disdain. "Welcome to Blackchapel," he said. "You're late."

25

Goosebumps prickled across Harry's skin as he was frogmarched through Blackchapel. The Ripper's Palace was a hymn to desecrated grandeur: its yawning hallways cobblestoned and stained with soot; its delicate chandeliers casting a sullen orange glow; its ceilings so high that fog swirled around the rafters. If it hadn't been for the malevolent presence of Lucien ahead of him and the ominous guard of the Bow Street Runners, then the journey would have been an occasion for wondrous awe.

The throne room was situated in the heart of the palace, a large circular room with arched windows and a raised platform at its centre, upon which rested a throne carved from smooth ebony. Lucien hobbled up to the dais and took a seat, Brick McNally standing at his side. The rest of the Runners fanned out across the room, blocking all the exits.

"I'm so glad you and your friends could join us, dear sister," Lucien proclaimed, settling back into his throne.

"Having left you buried beneath a building, I was as surprised as I was gladdened to hear that you had survived."

"I can imagine," Marianne replied acidly.

"After all, it gave me the chance to show you this." Lucien gestured around the throne room. "My seat of power. It seems only right that this place shall witness my final triumph over you. This time," he added menacingly, "you will not rise again."

"I'd be delighted to carry on from where we left off," drawled Marianne. "I'll fight you anywhere you like. But no doubt you'll rely on others to do your dirty work for you – as always."

"You mock me, Marianne?" Lucien leaned forward. "You should know better. You have faced me before, and bled at my hands. You know what I can become."

Marianne let out a peal of laughter. "The Black Phoenix? You sound so proud, brother. I have faced worse than that overgrown bird of yours – it holds no fear for me."

"Enough of this," spat Lucien. He turned to Brick McNally. "Kill them. Now."

There was the merest flicker of hesitation from the Chief Runner before he turned to his men and said: "You heard the order."

The brick golems plunged beneath the surface of the room, erupting amidst them in a single fountain of stone. The Runners dived in and out of the walls and the floor, turning the throne room into a writhing mass of stone fists and boots. Harry backflipped over a stone leg as it reached out to trip him up, then dodged out of the way as a hand shot out to grab his throat. Across the throne room, sparks flew from Marianne's sword as it rang against the Runners' hardened skin. Moving with a swift precision, she countered each attack as it speared out from the walls and the floor. But although she could block the golems, hurting them was another matter.

Lacking Harry and Marianne's agility, Carnegie was struggling to cope with the speed of the Runners' strikes. As he roared with anger, a golem shut up from out of the ground and dealt him a crunching blow in the ribs, sending him crashing into a table. With a howl of pain, the wereman picked up a bench and hurled it back at the Runner, who barely flinched as the wood splintered on its chest. The golem's hand shuddered, metamorphosing into a hammer. The two creatures raced forward to engage one another in a flurry of fluid bricks and sharp claws.

Out of the corner of his eye, Harry saw Raquella usher Sam behind a thick curtain. As a golem bore down upon them, the maid drew him away, running back towards the centre of the room.

"Look out!" she screamed.

Running at full tilt, the maid crashed into Harry, knocking both of them to the ground just as a stone pendulum swung down from the ceiling, whistling through the air where he had been standing. Feeling the earth tremble beneath him, Harry grabbed hold of Raquella and rolled to one side, narrowly avoiding a pillar of brick bursting up from the floor.

"This is hopeless!" he panted. "They're everywhere, and we can't even dent them!"

"So what are you going to do?" Raquella shouted back. "Give up?"

She dragged him back to his feet as another golem loomed up in front of them.

"HOLD!" a voice boomed out.

To Harry's surprise, everyone stopped. Even Carnegie stood back from his opponent, his face bruised and bleeding. Exhausted, Harry looked up to see a man standing in the doorway to the throne room, regally surveying the scene. Lucien stood up from his throne and peered into the gloom.

"Holborn?" he exclaimed sharply. "Where have you been? Why have the Runners stopped?"

"Because I commanded them to," the Abettor replied. "There is now a stronger power in this room than yours, cripple."

Holborn stepped forward into the light, revealing a bloodstained piece of rubble in his arms.

"It can't be!" Lucien gasped. "The Crimson Stone!"

The Abettor nodded. "Indeed. Whilst you have been destroying Darkside, I tracked down your forefather's most powerful artefact. Proof, if proof be needed, that I deserve to sit on that throne, not you."

Lucien's eyes narrowed. "You dare to challenge the Ripper?"

"You are no Ripper. Look – Marianne is alive! My claim is no less worthy than yours. Let me give you a demonstration."

As Holborn began murmuring to himself, behind him the curtain by the window twitched, and Sam ran out into the open.

"That's mine!" he shouted. "Give it back!"

The room watched dumbfounded as the boy reached up and snatched the Crimson Stone from Holborn. Ducking under the Abettor's despairing grasp, Sam sprinted for the door.

"Come back, Sam!" Raquella cried desperately. "You can save us! Control the Runners!"

But Sam kept running, disappearing through the archway and away into Blackchapel. As Holborn paled and edged back towards the doorway, the room was filled with the sound of mocking laughter.

"Oh, elegantly done, my loyal Abettor!" sneered Lucien. "Outwitted by a child. Not exactly behaviour becoming of a Ripper. Now both Darkside *and* the Stone will be mine. You won't even have the comfort of a quick death." Lucien snarled at Brick McNally. "What are you waiting for? Don't leave this room until all my enemies are dead!"

As the Ripper hobbled out of the throne room after Sam, the Runners turned back to face the rest of the group. It seemed there would be no escape after all. Harry squeezed Raquella's hand, and readied himself for the end.

*

Jonathan stumbled through the darkness after Holborn, feeling the tunnel wall with his hands as he went. His ribs were aching and his hands cut from where he had shifted the rubble from his body, but he was alive, a surge of hatred for the Abettor driving him onwards.

After what felt like miles of blind stumbling, Jonathan saw a shaft of pale light arcing down through a hole in the ceiling, illuminating a rickety wooden ladder. He stopped by the bottom rung, and cautiously scaled the ladder up into a draughty stone tower. With a shiver, he saw that he was surrounded by skeletal remains: rows of skulls and anguished piles of bones. It looked like the lair of some mythical monster that had been feasting on unwary travellers for centuries.

A trail of footprints was visible on the dusty floor, leading from the ladder to the door – Holborn's, Jonathan guessed. Unnerved by the lingering odour of death in the room, he hurried out of the building and into a melancholy garden, where the knotted undergrowth was coated in a deep layer of snow. A row of weeping willows swayed mournfully in the breeze. Holborn's footprints continued through the snow, skirting round the flower beds before coming to a halt at a door built into the high garden wall. The door was wide open: either the Abettor thought he had killed Jonathan in the cave-in, or he was in too much of a hurry to worry about him following.

Jonathan walked inside, heading up a narrow staircase and along the corridor beyond. Through the window, the broad thoroughfare of Pell Mell stretched out beneath him. The street was alive with an angry mob, Darksiders arguing and brawling with one another even as they swarmed up towards the dark outline of Blackchapel.

In the distance bright flames were flickering above the Grand, setting the night sky alight. The orange glow of the fires cast a fitful illumination over a series of grim portraits on the corridor wall, a gallery of cruel male faces sneering and glaring at any visitors who dared to go by. As Jonathan walked past them, he saw that each painting had a name written beneath it: Thomas, then George and Albert. The final portrait was larger than the others, and encased in an ornate wooden frame – beneath it, a note said simply "Jack".

A chill ran down Jonathan's spine. He was looking at Jack the Ripper: the founder of Darkside; Lightside's most notorious killer. He stared at the portrait, searching for traces of evil. A bespectacled face stared mildly back at him. Compared to the other grizzled Rippers, Jack looked more like a clerk than a murderer. It was only when Jonathan looked more closely and saw the cruel twist to the Ripper's mouth, and the soulless black pits of his eyes, that he could believe who this man was.

A thunderous explosion went off on Pell Mell, flooding the corridor with bright light. Jonathan turned to see three figures shuffling towards him, dragging their feet across the tiles. They were shirtless, exposing blackened masses of bruises and seeping pustules on their flesh. Drool dripped down from their slack mouths. Jonathan had spent enough time in Darkside to recognize ghouls when he saw them. Mindless undead cannibals, they roamed graveyards in search of food. No wonder Holborn hadn't been worried whether Jonathan had followed him or not.

With an angry groan, the ghouls lumbered towards him. What they lacked in speed, they more than made up for in strength. They could tear him apart with their bare hands. Jonathan turned to run in the opposite direction, only to see two more of the creatures walking up the steps from the garden.

Another explosion erupted outside, this one louder than the first. Even though the ghouls were slow, there wasn't enough room in the corridor to dodge round them. A tide of panic rose up within Jonathan. As he looked around frantically for a weapon, a black shape fluttered across his eye line, emitting a high-pitched squeaking noise. As he looked back the way it had come, he saw a churning black wave pouring down the corridor from the direction of the gardens, the shrill squeaking swelling to a roar.

Jonathan dropped to his knees and put his hands over his head.

The cloud of bats hit them like a hammer blow, submerging Jonathan and the ghouls in a blizzard of wings and claws. The ghouls groaned in confusion, their arms flailing as they were battered by the sheer mass of creatures. As he peered out between his fingers, Jonathan's heart sank at the sight of Vendetta striding through the storm. The vampire was carrying an épée in his hand, and on engaging the disoriented ghouls, the slender blade flashed again and again as he cut them down with a mixture of contempt and a deadly grace.

It was over in seconds. When the final ghoul dropped to the floor, Vendetta raised his hands in the air, and the bats drained back to the gardens as quickly as they had arrived. With the deafening squeaking abruptly gone, the silence throbbed in Jonathan's ears. He glanced up at the vampire, waiting for his blade to rise and fall one last time.

"Well, get up, then," Vendetta said irritably.

"What?" Jonathan replied, in disbelief.

"I'm not going to kill you," the vampire replied. "Yet. You're going to cause Lucien more problems alive than dead, so I'm going to have to forgo that particular pleasure for the time being."

Jonathan rose cautiously to his feet. "I guess I should say thank you," he said.

"Don't mention it." Vendetta pointed down the corridor. "Blackchapel is through there. Given the scenes of chaos outside, I suspect that the Bow Street Runners are protecting Lucien within the palace. Go cautiously."

"You're not coming with me?"

"Hardly. There are things I need to attend to here."

Jonathan looked down at the corpses littering the floor. "You're not going to stay and feed on those things, are you?"

Vendetta grimaced. "What a repulsive notion. Ghouls

don't bleed, not that I would touch their infested fluids even if they did. No, I have other priorities, Starling. Remember that we are only travelling in the same direction for a short time. If our paths should cross again, I won't show such restraint a second time."

The vampire spun on his heel and strode back towards the gardens. Jonathan watched him go, amazed that he was still alive. Taking a deep breath, he stepped over the ghoul corpses and carried on towards Blackchapel. After passing through a connecting door, he came out on to a landing at the top of a broad flight of stairs. Somewhere downstairs and to his left, a battle was raging: he could hear the ringing of blades and the rumbling of the Runners.

At the sound of footsteps, Jonathan pressed himself against the wall. He bit back an oath as Lucien limped quickly down the hallway and out through the doors, into the palace grounds. Wherever the Ripper was going, he was in a hurry.

Jonathan crept down the stairs, unsure of what to do. He could either head left, towards whoever or whatever was fighting, or head right in pursuit of Lucien. Torn, he glanced one way and then the other, then ran after the Ripper, praying to God that he had made the right choice.

26

Even as he repelled the latest strike from the Bow Street Runner, Elias Carnegie knew that he was doomed. The golem with the hammer hand had sought him out again – it showed no sign of pain; no weariness slowed its limbs. By contrast, each ragged breath hurt the wereman's bruised ribcage, and it was getting harder to dodge the blows.

As he pressed back against the wall, through the window Carnegie caught a glimpse of Lucien struggling through the snow in the palace grounds, chasing after Sam as the boy ran towards a small building by the perimeter wall. Several metres further back, the wereman saw Jonathan Starling ploughing resolutely after the Ripper.

"The boy's here!" Carnegie barked. "And he's gone after Lucien!"

Marianne had engaged two Runners, swaying out of harm's reach in time to the flow and ebb of their attacks. "Go and help him!" she shouted back.

"What? I'm not leaving you here!"

"We can't win this fight anyway!" Marianne cried. "Our only hope is the Crimson Stone. Go!"

There was a note of steely authority in the bounty hunter's voice that brooked no argument. As the Runner brought its hammer down, Carnegie stepped inside the swing and used the golem's momentum to throw it over his shoulder. The Runner disintegrated into pebbles as it hit the ground, re-forming almost immediately. Before it could come at him again, the wereman ran towards the window and hurled himself through it, shattering the glass into a thousand pieces. Landing on all fours in the snow, Carnegie howled with desire and began loping across the palace grounds.

Racing into the mausoleum behind Lucien, Jonathan found himself in a gloomy room, an army of lit candles casting a ghostly glow over the red marble walls. Above Jonathan's head, friezes depicted the final death throes of murder victims with a gory beauty. Beyond rows of pews, a statue of Jack the Ripper bestrode the room, black obsidian gleaming in the flickering candlelight.

At the back of the mausoleum, Sam lay passed out on the floor, the Crimson Stone lying just out of his grasp. The shock of being reunited with the artefact had overwhelmed the boy's mind. Lucien laughed as he limped towards him.

"Puny boy," he sneered. "The Stone is too powerful for children. Only a Ripper can truly wield such a talisman. You will bear witness to this fact only too soon."

"Leave him alone," Jonathan called out.

Lucien's head snapped round. "You!" he hissed, his eyes burning with hatred. "Must you haunt my every step?"

"It's over, Lucien," Jonathan said, trying to sound calm even though his pulse was racing. "None of your schemes have worked. Marianne is still alive. My mum survived the Bedlam. Darkside is uprising. And I won't let you get the Stone."

The Ripper smiled darkly. "Foolish child. You really think you can stop me? It's over? It has barely begun."

With that, Lucien's body began to tremble. Opening his throat, he let out a piercing, spine-tingling shriek. The Ripper fell to his knees, his skin rippling violently. He gasped in pain, and with the sound of cracking bones, two leathery wings erupted from his body. His face crumpled and twisted as a protruding beak began to grow out of it, whilst a covering of lank feathers swamped his flesh. Where before had stood a frail crippled man, a horribly majestic bird rose into the air. As shadows gathered around the bird, Jonathan felt a familiar shiver of dread run down his spine.

"Step aside, boy."

Elias Carnegie walked into the mausoleum. His clothes were torn, and his face was a mass of purple bruises. At the sight of the Black Phoenix, a flicker of grim amusement passed across his face.

"Always thought it would come back to you," he growled up at the bird.

"You know how strong that thing is, Carnegie!" Jonathan protested. "You can't fight it on your own!"

The wereman shot him a sideways glance. "Want to wager on that, boy?" Pushing his stovepipe hat back on his head and rolling up his sleeves, he continued in a conversational tone: "Before we begin, Lucien, I feel I should warn you: I play rough."

As the bird crowed with laughter, Carnegie bellowed and charged towards it. Jonathan watched helplessly as the two beasts clashed. The wereman was one of the most brutal fighters in Darkside, a savage hurricane of teeth and claws. But as Carnegie lunged at the Black Phoenix, aiming clubbing blows at his head, Jonathan knew that he didn't stand a chance. The bird effortlessly soared out of reach, its sinuous movements making Carnegie look clumsy in comparison.

A voice in Jonathan's head was screaming at him to run past the Phoenix and retrieve the Crimson Stone, but as the shadows around the bird thickened into an inky cloud, fear wrapped a frozen fist around Jonathan's heart. He drew back behind a pew, trying to fight the urge to burst into tears.

Carnegie fought on, undeterred. A vicious, feral creature with blobs of saliva dripping from his jaws, he had totally given in to the beast within. As the Phoenix dived towards him, Carnegie only just avoided a thrust from its deadly beak. He hit the deck, a stray talon knocking his stovepipe hat from his head and sending it rolling across the floor.

Jonathan had never seen the wereman move so quickly. His claws a blur, Carnegie aimed a slash across one of the bird's wings, drawing blood as he sliced open a vein. The Phoenix shrieked in pain, turned sharply in the air and nosedived towards the wereman. Forced back on to the defensive, Carnegie tried to block the attack, but the bird was too fast for him: with a caw of triumph, the Black Phoenix plunged all of its talons deep into the wereman's chest.

Carnegie froze, a shocked expression on his face. As the Black Phoenix withdrew its talons and rose back into the air, the wereman took a single tottering step forward, then collapsed to the floor of the mausoleum.

"No!" Jonathan screamed.

He broke from his cover and slid over to Carnegie, not caring whether the Phoenix attacked him or not. Tears welling in his eyes, he rolled the wereman over. Carnegie's chest was lacerated with dark, ugly wounds. The beast within him had subsided, leaving his craggy features looking all too human.

"Going to have to find some other idiot to get into trouble with now, boy," the wereman said faintly. He coughed, a trickle of dark blood running from his mouth.

"No!" sobbed Jonathan. "You can't leave me."

As his eyes began to roll up in his head, Carnegie mumbled something.

Jonathan leaned in closer. "What? I can't hear you."

"I said MOVE, boy!" Carnegie snarled. Summoning his last ounce of strength, the wereman shoved Jonathan to one side as the Black Phoenix swooped down from the air.

Jonathan rolled out of the way on pure instinct, crying out as a talon raked his side.

Overwhelmed by a mixture of pain, sorrow and anger, Jonathan felt the fog of fear lift. His mind suddenly clear, he saw the Crimson Stone on the floor in front of him.

Holborn crouched in the shadows behind the Ripper's throne, counting the paces to the nearest doorway. He had managed to hide as the golems had been distracted: first by Carnegie's dramatic exit, and now by Marianne. Even Holborn had to concede that the woman could fight. Shepherding the red-headed girl behind her, Marianne repelled the golems' shifting attacks, her fluorescent white hair blazing like a beacon as her sword whirled through the air.

Harry Pierce, however, was finished. No matter how bravely he had fought, the golems were too large and too powerful. Even as Holborn watched, a stray fist glanced off Harry's head, knocking him off his feet. The redhead screamed as the Runner leapt on Harry to finish him off.

"Nephew!" Marianne cried, desperately trying to battle her way towards him.

No, it wouldn't be long before the battle ended. Seizing his chance, the Abettor slipped out of the throne room and ran for his life.

The Black Phoenix screeched with rage as Jonathan scrabbled over to the Crimson Stone and picked it up.

Turning the talisman over in his hands, he was overwhelmed by the urge to destroy the accursed thing. At the same time, images of power flashed through his mind: Jonathan striding the halls of Blackchapel, servants pandering to his every whim; unruly crowds of Darksiders stopping and cheering his name as his carriage travelled through the borough; Jack the Ripper smiling and sweeping off his hat in greeting. . . With the Crimson Stone, he could bring down walls. He could crush his enemies between pillars of granite. He could take the throne for himself.

Instead, Jonathan began to run.

As he hurtled across the mausoleum, the shadow of the Phoenix fell over him, smothering him in nightmares. Jonathan ran through death and loneliness, pursued by bad memories: Alain's darkenings, when he had courted death time and again; the years Jonathan had spent wandering the streets of London, trying to lose himself in the crowds, riven by a sense that he didn't belong; the constant fear that his mum was dead. His heart was pounding so hard it was painful, his lungs were burning, and the marrow of his bones had turned to ice. But still Jonathan drove on, his legs moving of their own accord, even though he had no idea where to run. The Phoenix drew nearer, close enough for its foul, hot breath to burn the back of his neck.

Then the statue of Jack the Ripper loomed up in front of Jonathan, and suddenly he knew what to do.

As the Black Phoenix dived in for the kill, its razor-sharp beak arrowing towards his heart, Jonathan leapt into the air, every sinew in his body stretched to breaking point. At the height of his headlong dive, Jonathan drove the Crimson Stone down on to Jack's dagger. With a joyful singing sound, the obsidian blade sliced through the heart of the Stone, cleaving it in two.

There was a dazzling flash of white light, and a blast of energy that threw Jonathan halfway across the mausoleum. Half-blinded, he watched as the Black Phoenix flew straight into the inferno, and was incinerated in an explosion of pure light. The bird writhed in agony, tortured by the only flames it could not endure. It gave off the high-pitched squeal of an animal in pain, which deepened and swelled until it was Lucien's ragged screams echoing around the mausoleum.

With a final, mangled screech that was part-bird, part-human, the Black Phoenix tumbled to the ground. Its wings flapped feebly for one last time, and then it was still.

It was minutes before anyone stirred. Groggily raising his head, Jonathan stared at the bodies strewn across the mausoleum floor around him: the sizzling carcass of the Black Phoenix, Sam's slumped form and, worst of all, Carnegie's unmoving corpse. Jonathan's arms were numb and there was a terrible pain in his side, and at that moment in time he didn't want to be awake any more. Slumping back to the floor, he slipped gratefully into the arms of unconsciousness.

As he waited for the Runner to deliver the final blow, Harry threw his hands up in a futile attempt to shield his face. An image of his dead father appeared before his eyes. The thought of James waiting for him in the afterlife comforted him as a wall of bricks swung down towards him. He tensed in anticipation.

And then nothing happened.

Cautiously opening one eye, Harry looked up to see a giant fist paused inches from his face. There was a look of utter confusion etched on Brick McNally's features. Everywhere in the throne room, the Runners had stopped in their tracks, including the three looming over Marianne, who had been forced down on to one knee as she covered Raquella's shrinking form.

"They've stopped!" cried Harry. "What's happened?"

McNally frowned. "Someone has destroyed the Crimson Stone. The Ripper is no more." The Runner withdrew his fist and rumbled back into an upright pose. "We have no leader, no orders to follow any more. Our quarrel with you has ended."

"Well, I'll be damned," said Marianne, sheathing her sword with a merry zing. "Good old Jonathan!"

27

Aurelius Holborn raced along the Ripper's Corridor, his gold chains of office jangling against his chest. Even as he fled, his mind was still furiously calculating. Everything had gone wrong, his plans reduced to tatters. Whoever triumphed, either Lucien or Marianne, without the Crimson Stone there was no way Holborn could claim the throne. And if either of the Rippers got their hands on him, he was a dead man. There was no other option – he had to get out of Darkside.

Behind him, the sounds of fighting in Blackchapel had died away. It wouldn't be long before someone came looking for the Abettor. Maybe the Bow Street Runners had already been ordered after him. Spurred on by that thought, Holborn reached the end of the corridor and burst out into the gardens, his lungs on fire. It had been many years since the Abettor had been forced to run anywhere.

Bursting out into the deserted gardens, Holborn raced along the path, only to slip in the snowy mush and tumble to the ground. He dragged himself back to his feet, cursing as he brushed his ermine-lined cloak. As he staggered on, the Charnel House appeared out of the night, the tower set against the sky like a single stone finger. Holborn unlocked the door and peered cautiously inside. His heart leapt to see that the bone depository was empty. The trapdoor was only a few feet away, and beyond it the crossing point to Lightside. No one would find him there.

Holborn smiled. He wasn't finished yet.

"I was wondering when you'd get here."

The Abettor whirled round to see Vendetta emerging from the darkness.

"You!" Holborn hissed in horror. "What are you doing here?"

"I've been keeping an eye on proceedings. There are certain scores I have to settle. Accounts that require closing."

"Then you will know that the battle has ended," Holborn said, stalling. "More than likely, Lucien is back on the throne. You would be wise to leave Blackchapel before he finds you."

Vendetta didn't appear to be listening. "Do you know how many bodies I have drained?" he asked softly. "How many gallons of warm blood I have drunk? I have been dead for so many years. I have killed lords and ladies. Beggars and barrow boys. Enemies and associates alike. I have killed so often that it no longer gives me pleasure, only serves to quench my bloodthirst for a few more hours."

Reaching into his waistcoat, the vampire drew out a small dagger. The Abettor began to back away.

"Think, Vendetta!" he cried desperately. "Think what we could achieve if we joined forces. Together, we could rule Darkside!"

Vendetta ignored him. "But killing you, Holborn, ah . . . now that would bring me a joy so pure that I will be desolate when it is eventually over."

As the vampire advanced, Holborn's feet went out from beneath him, and he toppled over backwards. He landed with a loud rattle on his back, on top of a pile of musty bones. He had fallen into one of the Charnel House pits.

Vendetta appeared at the edge, and looked down at him with icy amusement.

"How very helpful of you."

"Please," the Abettor cried, holding his hands out. "Spare me – I beg you!"

His fangs flashing in the darkness, Vendetta fell upon Holborn like the night, and the Charnel House echoed to the sound of lingering screams.

Jonathan awoke to see Marianne's pale face looking down at him. For a few seconds he wasn't sure where he was; then the memory of Carnegie's death flooded back and he began to cry.

"Oh, Jonathan," Marianne said quietly. "I am sorry. What happened?"

"The Black Phoenix was going to kill me," he replied miserably. "Carnegie saved me."

"That makes sense. He always was too brave for his own good. And stubborn with it."

Jonathan glanced over at the wereman's body. "I just can't believe he's gone."

"I've seen friends die in battle," said Marianne sympathetically. "Those wounds take the longest to heal. But remember one thing: it took Darkside's very worst to kill him. If Carnegie could have chosen a way to go, it would have been like this. Saving you. Of that you can be sure."

"Maybe you're right," sniffed Jonathan. "I don't know. . . I can't think straight right now. Could you leave me with him – just for a bit?"

Marianne squeezed him gently on the shoulder, and left him to grieve.

Jonathan stayed by Carnegie for the rest of the night, nurturing an impossible hope of seeing a muscle twitch or a breath disturb the ribcage. Then, as the day began to dawn, in his head he heard a voice growling at him: *Enough tears, boy. Everyone moves on in the end*. Carnegie would be embarrassed to see him like this, Jonathan knew. He owed it to the wereman to move, no matter how heavy his heart.

Wiping his eyes on his sleeve, Jonathan stood up. He walked over to Jack's statue and retrieved Carnegie's stovepipe hat from where it had fallen, before placing it carefully on the wereman's chest.

"Goodbye, Carnegie," he said, and walked out of the mausoleum.

The day dawned grimly, beneath grey skies filled with leaden clouds. In the throne room, the aftermath of battle hung heavily in the air. Marianne paced thoughtfully up and down the room, past an impassive platoon of Bow Street Runners. She had carried the unconscious Sam back from the mausoleum, laying the boy down on a bench to recover as she solemnly announced Carnegie's death.

Raquella's face had streaked with tears as she'd tried to come to terms with the news. Harry had wrapped a comforting arm around her and was staring moodily out of the window.

"It's started to rain," he said.

"Good." Marianne pointed to the thick plumes of smoke visible above the palace walls. "The Grand is still burning. The rain should help put it out."

"Are they still rioting on the streets?"

There was a rumble of rubble from behind Harry. "Not any more," said Brick McNally. "Didn't you hear the Blackchapel Bell tolling? The people know that Lucien is dead. They are concentrating on putting out the fires."

As Jonathan slowly entered the throne room, a respectful silence descended upon the room. Raquella stood up and gave him a fierce hug.

"Are you all right?" she asked.

"Not really," replied Jonathan. "But if there's one thing I

know, it's that Carnegie wouldn't want us to fall apart because of him. So what do we do now?"

It was McNally who answered, in a grating voice. "Darkside needs a Ripper. You must choose one." He turned and fixed his gaze on Marianne. "You are the rightful heir, are you not? You must take the throne."

There was an expectant pause. The bounty hunter smiled.

"Charming offer," she said mildly. "But one I'll have to turn down, I'm afraid."

Surprise rippled across McNally's face. "You don't want to be the next Ripper?"

"It's rather lost its appeal," Marianne replied breezily. "The thought of spending my days rattling around this dreary place with only the ghosts of my murderous ancestors for company is not a happy one. Life's too short, don't you think?"

"Marianne!" protested Harry. "You can't turn it down! If you don't become the Ripper, who will?"

"That's the silliest question you've asked, nephew," said Marianne, with a chime of laughter. "You, of course."

Harry blinked. "Me?"

"Who else? If Lucien hadn't murdered your father, he would probably have won the Blood Succession, and you would have been next in line anyway. This rights an old wrong. So how about it, Harry?"

The young man didn't reply, biting his lip in hesitation.

"Oh for goodness' sake, Harry!" Raquella said briskly.

"What are you waiting for? Of course you should do it. It's your birthright!"

He turned and gave the maid a wry glance. "Well, if you put it like that," he said, a note of amusement in his voice. "How can I say no?"

"Good for you," Marianne said approvingly. "I have a feeling you'll be rather good at it." She glanced over at Brick McNally. "Do we have the support of the Bow Street Runners?"

The golem bowed his head at Harry. "The Runners always obey the will of the Ripper. He should take his rightful place."

McNally gestured towards the ebony throne on top of the dais. His face pale, Harry walked slowly up the steps and cautiously settled himself down into the seat.

"How does it feel up there?" Jonathan asked.

"I guess I'll get used to it," Harry replied. "What now?"

"First things first," Brick McNally replied. The golem extended a finger towards Jonathan. "What do you want us to do with him?"

"What do you mean?" Harry asked, frowning.

"He destroyed the Crimson Stone. A grievous crime, whether a friend or not."

Harry drew himself up in his seat. "No one touches Jonathan. I am the Ripper now – that is a direct order."

"As you wish," the golem said, in a spray of soot. "Do you require anything else from us?"

"I think you've been on the streets for too long," Harry

replied. "Return to the gardens, and let's hope your rest isn't disturbed for a long time."

McNally nodded. "It is done," he said simply.

As one, the platoon of Runners dissolved thunderously into the ground, leaving the walls of the throne room trembling, and the new Ripper alone to face the future.

28

For two days a curtain of rain fell upon Darkside, dampening down the smouldering embers of the Grand and submerging the cobbled streets in water. When the deluge finally slackened to a drizzle, the gates to Blackchapel creaked open, and a small procession began walking in the direction of Bleakmoor's forbidding hills. The mood was one of sombre silence, all eyes fixed on the plain wooden coffin at the head of the cortege.

As word spread of the mourners' passage, crowds quickly formed on the pavements. Although funeral processions were an all-too-frequent part of Darkside life, this was different. For one thing, the new Ripper was present – and was even helping to carry the coffin, an unheard-of honour. People pointed and whispered at one another as Harry passed. Despite his young age, they noted his broad shoulders and sober bearing with approval. He was sure to be an improvement on his predecessor.

The sudden end to Lucien's regime had surprised the

borough's denizens as much as it had pleased them. Following the announcement of Harry's accession to the throne, all sorts of wild rumours had flown around Darkside. Some – clearly those among the borough's more unstable or gullible elements – had whispered that the Crimson Stone had been returned to Blackchapel, only to be destroyed. The regulars in the Rook I'th Vine alehouse had snorted into their mugs of beer hearing that one. They were too long in the tooth to believe in fairy tales.

On the other side of Carnegie's coffin from Harry, Jonathan kept his head held high and tried not to think about the wereman's lifeless body inside. He had spent the previous two days holed up in Blackchapel, wandering the draughty palace in a numb daze as the wind and rain buffeted the walls outside. Over a subdued dinner, Harry had cautiously brought up the issue of Carnegie's burial, and where it should take place. Jonathan had known the answer immediately.

"We should bury him on Bleakmoor," he said. "That's what he would have wanted."

"You think?"

It was Raquella who nodded. "Elias loved to roam up there. It was the wildest part of Darkside, after all."

"Then Bleakmoor it is," Harry declared.

Now the procession wound through the foothills, making its way towards a spot on the brow of the hill that provided a sweeping view of Darkside in all its grimy, smog-ridden majesty. The way was steep, the footing treacherous in the long, straggly grass. The winter sun, barely visible for days, was slumping towards the skyline, and the shadows were lengthening across the hillside.

Despite the creeping gloom, Jonathan took heart from the sight of his mum and dad walking hand in hand nearby. Theresa and Alain had arrived at Blackchapel a couple of hours beforehand, rolling up to the gates in one of Vendetta's carriages. It turned out that Raquella had sent a messenger back to Lightside to relay the sad tidings, and organized transport for them in time for the funeral. Although at first Jonathan was worried at the sight of Alain returning to the borough so soon after a darkening, looking at their faces he knew that nothing could have kept them away.

What Vendetta had made of Raquella's activities remained open to debate. The vampire had vanished again – although reports had filtered back to Blackchapel that the curtains of his mansion were now drawn again during the daytime, and a giant bonfire of Holborn's possessions had been burned on the back lawn. The Heights was Vendetta's once more.

The procession came to a halt by a simple hole on the edge of the hillside, the pallbearers placing the coffin gently down on to the ground. Looking around the assembled crowd, Jonathan was amazed by how many familiar faces he saw. At the head of the mourners stood Arthur Blake, the newly reinstated editor of the *Darkside Informer*. The portly man was accompanied by his ward Clara, an orphan Harry and Raquella had rescued from the No'Penny Poorhouse. Beside the editor, Jonathan recognized the Queenpin, the beautiful, dark-skinned mistress of Slattern Gardens, who had shared a mysterious history with Carnegie. Tears glistened in her eyes like jewels. Even Darkside's finest burglars, the Troupe, had come to pay their respects. Jonathan couldn't help but notice that they were dressed smartly, their expensive clothes dappled with diamonds and other gems. Business was clearly good. The leader of the Troupe, Antonio Correlli, nodded solemnly at Jonathan as their eyes met.

Happily, Samuel Northwich was also present. On waking up a day after the battle in Blackchapel, it quickly became clear that the destruction of the Crimson Stone had cleared the boy's mind. Now clean and well-dressed, Sam looked like the bright magician's assistant Jonathan and Raquella had first encountered.

A respectful hush settled over the crowd as Carnegie's remains were lowered into the ground, and a pair of gravediggers began piling earth over the wereman's coffin. For a few seconds the only sound was the thud of shovelled soil, and then a piercing howl rang out over Bleakmoor: a lone cry suddenly joined by another, and then another, until the hills echoed to a chorus of baying.

"Wolves," Jonathan whispered, shivering at the sound.

The howling continued until the last of the soil had been patted down on Carnegie's grave – then it came to an abrupt halt, as though an invisible conductor had lain down his baton. As Jonathan bowed his head and said a silent farewell to his friend, he was suddenly aware of Raquella and Harry standing next to him. The red-headed maid was dabbing at her eyes with a handkerchief, while the new Ripper had a protective arm around her shoulder.

Raquella stepped forward and squeezed Jonathan tightly. "Thank you," she whispered.

"Thank *you*," Jonathan whispered back. "We did all right in the end, didn't we?"

She nodded quickly.

"I was amazed to see your master didn't show up," Jonathan said wryly.

"No," replied Raquella. "That is not Vendetta's way." She paused. "And he is no longer my master."

"You've finally left him?"

"In a manner of speaking. I'm leaving the Heights. Vendetta has offered me a position at his bank."

"You must be joking!" Jonathan said incredulously. "You're going to keep working for him?"

"I think he has realized that I can help him with more than laundering and polishing silver. It is in his interest to take care of me."

"You can say that again," Harry said darkly. "I'll be keeping a very close eye on that vampire." The Ripper took Jonathan's hand and shook it warmly. "Any time you come back to Darkside, you'll be welcome at Blackchapel. An honoured guest of the Ripper."

"Thanks. Good luck with, you know, being in charge."

"I'm going to need it," laughed Harry. "Sure you don't fancy being my Abettor?"

Jonathan gave him a rueful smile. "I think I've had enough trouble for the time being."

"Well, it's an open offer. Take care, my friend."

After a final embrace they parted company, the rotten borough's new ruler leaving hand-in-hand with the Bank of Darkside's new clerk. The sky had darkened, and the air was filling with raindrops again. Eager to escape the threatening storm clouds, the mourners began to make their way back towards Darkside. Jonathan was about to follow suit when he had the sudden sensation that he was being watched. He turned and scanned Bleakmoor through the rain.

Along the brow of the hill, removed from all the other mourners, a figure was standing beneath the twisted boughs of a tree. Dressed in all black, she sheltered beneath a large umbrella that spread out above her head like the wings of a giant bat. As he stared at the figure, Jonathan caught a sudden glimpse of flourescent-pink hair. He smiled.

"Are you coming, Jonathan?" he heard Alain call over to him.

"In a minute," he replied. "I'll catch you up."

Leaving the rest of the crowd behind him, Jonathan fought through the tangled grass to the brow of the hill, where Marianne Ripper stood waiting for him. She still bore the scars of battle, her pale face bruised and cut. A half-smile danced over her lips as Jonathan approached.

"Looked like a nice service," she called out.

"You should have joined us," Jonathan replied.

Marianne made a face. "I'm not a fan of funerals. Thank goodness I won't be around to see mine."

The wind picked up, sending a lock of pink hair whipping across her face. She tucked it back behind her ear. Jonathan was aware of the faint smell of perfume hanging between them – although he was fairly certain that this time it wasn't the one with the hypnotic powers, it was still vaguely distracting.

"So what are you going to do now?" Marianne asked.

"I'm leaving with my mum and dad. Going back home to try to live as a normal family – if that's possible. I guess they'll make me finish school as well."

"Back to Lightside for good, then?"

Jonathan nodded. "My mum can cope with the atmosphere there, at least for now, and my dad can't take living on Darkside any more. What about you – what are you going to do? I thought you'd be back with Humble and Skeet."

Marianne shook her head. "I'm thinking about a change of career. I'm bored of bounty hunting." She grinned mischievously. "Actually, I was thinking about becoming a private detective."

"You're kidding me!"

"It makes perfect sense to me. This place is always going to need private detectives, and given that it's just lost its finest. . ." She paused. "What do you think Carnegie would say?"

Jonathan laughed. "Honestly? I think he'd go nuts."

"I think you're probably right." She paused delicately. "I could do with a partner, you know. Someone with relevant experience of the profession."

"Oh." Jonathan tapped his foot, pretending to think. "Not many of them around, I'd guess."

"Not really."

"I suppose . . . well, if you did need a partner, I'll be coming back here one day. You'd have to wait for a while, though. Would you?"

An odd look passed over Marianne's face. She looked away, over Bleakmoor's wild expanse.

"For you, Jonathan Starling? I suppose I could wait."

Before he could say anything else, Marianne nodded briskly at the trail of people disappearing out of sight over the brow of the hill.

"I'd go after them if I were you," she said. "It's starting to get dark, and you wouldn't want to be up here on your own after nightfall. There are some dangerous things about."

"What about you – are you going to be OK?"

Marianne gave out a silvery laugh. "I'm hurt, Jonathan! I *am* one of those dangerous things."

She leaned forward and kissed him softly on the cheek. For a brief second Jonathan found himself enveloped in her perfume, and he was less sure than ever that it didn't have special powers. By the time he had come out of his daze, Marianne was already striding away across the moor, her umbrella resting upon her shoulder.

"See you around some time!" she called out.

Jonathan watched Marianne walk away along the hill's ridge, until the last shock of fluorescent hair had been swallowed up by the gloom. "I guess you will," he murmured.

Far away below him, the street lamps of Darkside were beginning to wink into life. It wouldn't be long before the denizens of the rotten borough would emerge from their houses on to the streets, lured out by the promise of shady deals and secret plots; jingling pockets that were ripe for picking; gullible minds begging to be sweet-talked and swindled. Thieves and murderers; criminals to the last man and woman.

Turning on his heel, Jonathan began striding through the tangled grass back towards the black heart of Darkside.

Acknowledgements

I n the writing of this series I've racked up some fairly hefty personal debts, so I'd better settle my accounts here, before my creditors turn ugly and start reaching for their weapons. . .

Heartfelt thanks to everyone at Scholastic – past and present – for supporting the series and turning my tatty manuscripts into something resembling proper books: in particular, Elv and Zöe for their frankly brutal reigns of editorial terror; Laura and Jess for their razor-sharp copy-edits; and all the publicity staff who've had the misfortune of dealing with me over the years. Also, a special mention to Studio Spooky for five fantastically creepy covers.

Beyond the ramparts of Scholastic Towers, I'd like to express my deep gratitude to Reg and Richard for being crazy enough to back both me and *Darkside*, and to Ben for his timely and frequent offerings of inspiration.

Finally, love to all my family and friends, who have

endured countless rambling monologues about vampires and plot crises, added children's books to already groaning shelves, and generally helped to stave off the madness for another year. The final word – perhaps inevitably – goes to Lieven, Belgium's finest zoo buddy.

Catch up on all the Darkside adventures, now with a terrifying new look

Jonathan's home has been attacked. His dad's in an asylum. He's running for his life. And there's nowhere to hide.

He's stumbled on the city's greatest secret: Darkside.

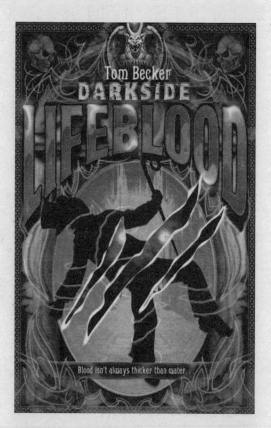

A brutal killer is on the loose!

When Jonathan and Carnegie agree to investigate a series of vicious murders in Darkside, they don't realize what they've stumbled into. Jonathan soon discovers his mother was investigating a similar crime on the day she disappeared, and the trail starts to lead uncomfortably close to home.

Before long he finds himself embroiled in the borough's most dangerous secret – and its most dangerous family.

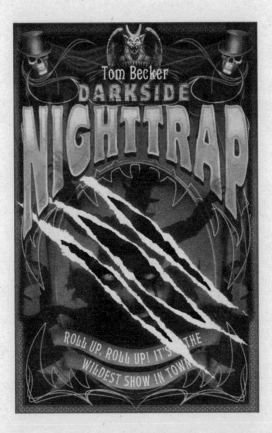

ROLL UP, ROLL UP! IT'S THE WILDEST SHOW IN TOWN

Mrs Elwood has been kidnapped!

Jonathan will do anything to get her back, even if it means breaking into the home of one of Darkside's most notorious criminals. The plan's in place for a dangerous heist – but is this mission impossible from the start?

Tom Becker

DARKSIDE

TIMECURSE

EVERY SECOND COUNTS...

In the midst of a bloodthirsty power struggle,
Jonathan must find out the secret of a mysterious watch – and
avoid getting killed while he does it. Along the way,
he'll finally discover the answer to the question
that's been haunting him for years:

Could his mother still be alive?